CRUMPLED

STORIES FROM THE HORROR ARCHIVES

Edited by Jyl Glenn

Paperback ISBN: 979-8-9919908-0-6

Cover Artist: Savannah R. Fischer

Editor: Jyl Glenn

Interior Formatting: Jyl Glenn

First edition 2024

Signatures

Savannah R. Fischer	Derek Thomas
Kate Reedwood	Andy Edge
Kristal Shanahan	Kimberly Nicole
AJ Humphreys	Joseph Murnane
Svea Neitzke	David K. Slater
Jacinta Rae	Dylan Wells
Mel Kitching	Ali Toothman
Jules Terry	Chris Heinicke
Denver Wheeler	K.L. Allister

Jyl Glenn

Dedicated to Lord Fungini and every writer who has ever had a story rejected.

Credit: Jules Terry

CONTENTS

INTRODUCTION

I love a well-worn paperback, the kind that appears as if it had sat on a grenade. The stale yellow paper, cracked spine, bent edges, and faded price tags all add to the book's character. It's seen some things, and I get a weird sense of enjoyment trying to envision its history. How many hands held it? How many people loved it, and how many couldn't stand it? How many receipts and wrappers acted as bookmarks crushed between its pages?

It's easy to see the life of a novel. The scrapes and bruises give you an idea of its life. Stories themselves don't show those scars, but so often, a piece of fiction has fought through years of battle too.

As soon as an author completes a story, they have to edit it. Then, they have to edit it and edit it and edit it. If they haven't beaten the story into extinction, it goes to beta readers who provide feedback, and then, you guessed it, it gets edited again.

At this point, a large percentage of stories face their first rejection, the one that comes from the author themselves. Ask any author how many completed stories they have sitting in random files on their computer. Maybe, though, the author pushes through, they check out the market, debate on where the story best fits, and ship it off to a thing called the slush pile.

A publisher sifts through upwards of thousands of submissions and rejects most of them. The author, sometimes waiting for weeks or even months for a response, clicks open their email to discover a form rejection, which is a simple, "Sorry, it's not for us right now, but try submitting something else down the line."

If the author truly believes in this story, they'll go back to the internet to hunt down other markets and go through the whole process all over again. Stephen King notoriously pegged his rejections to a railroad spike he'd stabbed into his wall. I remember one author telling me he had 67 rejections for a short story that he finally got published. That story ended up nominated for a Bram Stoker Award.

This isn't always the lifeline of a story, of course. Sometimes the author themselves reject the story, and then years later, they find it buried in a file somewhere, discover it had the bones of something promising, and they rewrite it, polish it, make it shine. Maybe they combine a few stories to fill in the weak spots. Maybe they reject it for a second time before finding it years later and trying all over again.

I have stories I've tried to write for over a decade. Once in a while, I open them up, and wrestle with them again until the damned thing pins me back down until I tap out.

The point here is that when you read a story, it's more than just a combination of words put together haphazardly. It's seen some things. The story has its own story. Someone sat on the other side of a screen and bled for it.

The book you hold in your hand is born from this idea. It's stories that have faced turmoil and made it out the other side, ready to be given another chance.

But, as I said, all stories have their own story, and this one is quite unique. You see, anthologies are typically put together in one of two ways. Either they are invite only, where the publisher invites the authors they know would fit the theme, or they're through submissions, which I've explained above. This one was born a different way.

A while back, a group of authors got together and formed a collective. Most of them were newer to publishing, but not all. They had a few goals when forming this group. To help each other grow as artists, to look out for each other, to encourage and critique each other. They became fast friends, and together, they've accomplished an astounding amount in a very short time. Someday, a good lot of them will be legends in the genre.

This anthology is theirs. It was their way of working together on a project and producing something as a collective. And what better way to represent that than with a series of stories that once faced rejection. It's a great way to say, "Hey, we've all had our struggles, but we are better together. And together, we can take these rejected works and make them shine."

You'll find a lot of horrors in this book. Greek Gods, terrifying crustaceans, kidnappings, shedding skin, creepy dolls, revenge, angry ghosts, cults, murderers, and even an evil Santa and a creepy raccoon. All of these stories feature a unique voice, a different storyteller looking to make their mark in the world of horror, and all of them have faced rejection.

These stories have stories. Like some of the protagonists in these tales, they fought against the darkness, clawed from the dirt, faced the hauntings, wielded their powers, and kept going.

At one time, they haunted the author. But then the authors found their tribe, and together they exorcized their demons, and put those stories out there so they could do one thing: Haunt you. The curse has been passed. It's yours now.

I hope you take this book, bend its spine, dog-ear the pages, show it some love. I hope it finds a new home, and a new one, and a new one until one day, I stumble on the paperback in a used bookstore and smile. Because I know this one, and it's seen some things.

Gage Greenwood
01/06/2025

Daughters of Terpsichore

by Savannah R. Fischer

Ioanna glanced toward the menacing ship, THE MEDUSA, its reflection in the midnight water lit ominously by the moon. A wooden bust of its namesake hung from the prow, attempting to frighten off any malignant spirits. Shuddering, she braced herself for the journey ahead. Her father meant to bring her aboard; ferry her across the sea to some foreign land, where he would marry her off to whoever would offer the highest bride price for her. She did not want to go, but as a woman, she had no choice. Stepping onto the gangplank, she crept aboard, hoping to make her way to her cabin before she could be accosted by a member of the crew. Without the benefit of her father's protection, she was at their mercy. She breathed a brief sigh of relief when she made it aboard. The first battle, however minor it may seem, had been won. The smell of the fresh sea air calmed her.

As she made her way to her cabin, she reflected on earlier in her day. Her mother took her to the temples of the old gods to pray and offer tribute. They visited Poseidon, god of the sea, to ask for safe travels. This was followed by Hera, the goddess of women and marriage, to ask for her blessing and a good, gentle husband. They visited Athena, asking for wisdom for her father, and finally, her favorite, Artemis. She fell on her knees, begging the goddess to preserve her chastity, and to hunt down those who may wish to cause her harm. Satisfied she had done what she could, her mother pressed her letter opener into her hands. "For protection," she whispered.

Close to her cabin, she heard a ruckus from the captain's quarters. She pressed her ear to the door, hoping to glean information about her father's activities. Her labors were not in vain. She heard her father with what she assumed to be a local tavern girl. He abided by the motto, "a whore in every port." She could hear the woman gagging as her father proudly proclaimed, "That be it, wench. Choke on it." Disgusted, she turned away. Leave it to her father to choose to cavort with a common whore over making sure his own daughter made it aboard the ship safely. Making it to her cabin, she stood stunned at the sight of another woman in her bed.

Ioanna's cheeks flamed as she took in the lovely woman before her. Lit by the candlelight, her hair fell in waves around her shoulders, framing a kind face. "I'm María. We are to be bunk mates I have been told." Ioanna knew better than to question anything aboard the ship, so she simply nodded and bedded down for the night.

Over the following days, the two women struck up a fast friendship. The crew paid them no mind as it was known Ioanna, and by extension her friend María, was untouchable. María also traveled to be sold into marriage, a fate the two women lamented over together. Alone in their room, their nights began to transform from worry over their intended husbands to more impure thoughts. María made the first move, taking Ioanna's hand in hers and planting a gentle kiss on her lips.

Surprised, Ioanna recoiled. Noting the hurt in María's eyes, she spoke. "I'm sorry, María. I was just surprised. We could get in a lot of trouble if the crew finds us."

"I could get in trouble, Ioanna. Not you. With your father as captain, you are untouchable. I don't know how much time we have left on our journey, or what the future holds, but I know now, in this moment, I want to be with you." Overcome with passion, the two tumbled into bed together, consummating their forbidden love. They continued in this fashion for weeks until the storm came.

One fateful night, a storm brought on by Poseidon's wrath assaulted the ship. Rain pelted the deck like tears of an angry goddess, sending all but the most necessary crew members scuttling deep into the bowels of the ship. The captain struggled to be heard over the squall, bellowing, "Steady now, men, we mus' stay our course!" As the wind whipped through the rigging and sails, it combined with the rain and the crashing of the onslaught of waves to make a dissonant chord. Fear struck deep into the hearts of everyone on board, except the two young women, nestled together below deck.

In her private cabin, Ioanna held fast to her secret paramour, María. The only two women on board, they formed a steadfast bond. Their love grew as vast as the sea, but they knew they could never be discovered for fear of retaliation from the crew. As the daughter of the captain, Ioanna had protection, but there would be no such thing for María.

The lone candle sputtered out, leaving the lovers enshrouded in darkness. Ioanna rested her head on María's chest, relishing in its simple rise and fall with every breath.

María ran her hands through Ioanna's short hair before planting a kiss on the crown of the woman's head. Although Ioanna often rebuffed her remarks, María truly believed her to be the most beautiful woman she ever laid eyes on, or lain with. Secure in the cabin, the women began to make love.

BANG! The door burst open, startling the lovers. "Cap'n says," the first mate paused as his lantern illuminated the scene. "Well, well, well...wha' do we 'ave 'ere?" The women scrambled to cover themselves as two crew members stomped into the cabin. Each woman felt herself grabbed by the arms as they were wrenched apart. The men laughed as they forced their disheveled prizes to the deck.

"Cap'n," screamed the first mate, "we caught dese 'er whores ca'vortin' down below." The captain's eyes turned thunderous as he turned to look at the women. He took in their disheveled appearance and the tears streaming down their faces and knew the accusations to be true.

"Do what must be done," he commanded without a second look at his daughter. The first mate, holding María, began to walk the woman toward the dangerous edge of the ship, eliciting screams from both women. Ioanna head-butted the man holding her captive, breaking his nose. He howled as he instinctively brought his hands to quench the spurting blood, releasing Ioanna from this grasp. She made to run for María, but another member of the crew stood in her way. He backhanded her, the blow severe enough it brought her to her knees. Her head swam, but she continued to crawl toward the screaming and struggling María.

María's screams reached a fever pitch as the first mate lifted her into the air. Her eyes met Ioanna's, and she mouthed, "I love you." Then the man heaved and mercilessly tossed her overboard into the frothing waves. Ioanna ran to the edge, but María was already lost in the undulating water.

"Take her back to her cabin and lock the door," said the captain. "'Tis time this willful daughter o'mine learned her place." Sobbing, Ioanna allowed herself to be carted back to her room. The crewman threw her forcefully onto the bed and locked the door. Heartbroken, Ioanna burrowed into her blanket, still covered in María's perfumed scent, and sobbed until morning.

Ioanna woke up bleary-eyed, unsure of when her tears had finally exhausted her to the point of fitful slumber. María's scream of terror as she went overboard haunted her. An intense need to urinate forced her out of bed. She hastily utilized the chamber pot before attempting to leave her room. It was time to confront her father about the atrocities he allowed under his command. She rattled the cabin door, startled to find it locked from the outside. She banged on the door, but she was either ignored or the sound was lost among the thumping of the waves. Ioanna bet it was the former, a type of punishment. Her father had probably taken last night's display as a personal affront to his dignity. He made his desire to marry her off, no, sell her off, to a wealthy merchant perfectly clear. She always knew in her heart of hearts he did not view her as a daughter in terms of love. To him, she served only as a means to spin a tidy profit.

Resigned to being left alone for an indeterminate amount of time, Ioanna sat down on her bed. She gathered the blanket to her face, attempting to reminisce on happier times.

Instead, her memory assaulted her. She pressed her hands to her temples, trying to stop the horrible images from flashing through her mind. María being grabbed from her. María being hauled to the upper deck. María saying she loved her. María being thrown overboard. It was too much for her heart to bear.

She reached into her bedside table and found the decorative letter opener her mother gave her. The intent was to protect herself from drunken sailors with their sights on the captain's daughter. Its long, thin shaft glinted in the meager light from the cabin's paltry porthole. With a shuddering breath, she lifted its point to rest between her breasts. *THUMP!* Ioanna dropped the letter opener, opening a small wound, which began to bleed. Ioanna didn't notice. *THUMP!*

She took a quick inventory of her surroundings. The noise obviously did not come from the door, and it didn't sound like anything she heard before. It was not a fist pummeling the wall or door, nor cargo sliding around and bumping into things. *THUMP! THUMP!* This time, the sound felt demanding, almost as if someone tried to get Ioanna's attention. Turning her attention to the only possible explanation, Ioanna looked at the porthole. She instantly recoiled.

A hand, covered with scales and tipped with dangerous black talons, sat framed in the narrow pane of glass. She waged an internal war before deciding to approach the porthole. What she saw took her breath away. On the ring finger gleamed a simple gold band, a token María wore. *This can't be*, thought Ioanna, before a voice slithered into her mind.

"Ioanna," whispered the voice, "they killed me, Ioanna. This whole damn ship must pay for their crimes." Ioanna trembled. The voice resembled María's, but yet not. The tone was wrong, darker, sultry even, with just a touch of malice. Ioanna pinched herself, willing herself to wake up from this nightmare. The hand disappeared from the glass, and she began to breathe a sigh of relief. The sigh quickly turned into a startled shriek as a face filled the glass pane.

There, framed in the porthole, swam a reborn, twisted version of María. Her skin glistened in iridescent gray scales, mimicking the Tahitian pearls Ioanna heard of. Her attempt at a smile revealed obsidian fangs, tapered to perfect points for rending the flesh of those who wronged her. But the most disturbing change was her eyes. María always had the most beautiful emerald eyes, but they were transformed into two coal black pits.

The voice returned, less harsh this time. Instead, it enveloped Ioanna like a lover's embrace, warm and tender. "Ioanna, please...help me. We can be together again." Ioanna's eyes widened.

"Together? But how? I watched you drown!"

"Oh, Ioanna, Terpsichore bargained with Poseidon and Hades and claimed me as her own." Ioanna stood speechless. "The deal was simple. I would become one of Terpsichore's children, and I would bring this ship to its watery grave." María pulled her disfigured face back from the glass, giving a glimpse of her long, supple tail, before gently placing her hand against the glass. "Together?"

Ioanna took a deep breath, steadying herself. She raised her petite hand to the pane, so close to her love she could almost imagine the feel of the scales, and whispered, "Together."

Ioanna sat back on her bed, a dagger now grasped in her hands. María guided her to the weapon before giving her instructions.

Shakily, she made the first cut, slicing between her second and third toes. White hot pain sluiced through her as the dagger sliced through flesh, igniting her nerves, and with enough force, severing even bone. Every inch brought with it searing agony as her sheets became drenched in shimmering crimson. The blade continued, separating her foot in two up to the ankle. Dizzy with pain, Ioanna could see the innermost recesses of her ruined foot, splayed for the love of her new patron goddess, Terpsichore, mother of sirens. Hardening herself for the task at hand, she took a needle and thread she kept for sewing and stitched the incisions. Working piece by bloody piece, she stitched until her foot resembled a split fin. The pain lanced through her in excruciating waves, but she was heartened knowing her goddess smiled upon her. Outside, María began to sing.

Once a maiden with no voice, María now sang with a voice unparalleled by even the angels. It rose and fell with the waves, snagging the hearts of every man onboard. "It be a siren," a crewmember yelled, but not before a splash echoed off the side of the ship. A man dove overboard, thrashing against the waves as he made for María. He swam relentlessly, finally reaching her. She enveloped him in her loving embrace, pulling him in for a passionate kiss. But as their lips touched, the man let out an ear-splitting shriek. His lips hung loose, pried from his face by María's fangs. Whatever illusion he was under fell away, and his shrieks intensified as he took in the siren before him.

Leering hungrily, María sank her claws and fangs into her unwitting victim. Her claws raked into his back, holding him agonizingly in place while weeping blood into the ocean. She finished sundering his lips from his face, then moved to his nose and cheeks. Her tongue darted out, prizing the man's eye from its socket. She savored the first orb, and then the second, like the sweetest of candies. Nerve endings dangled like bloody noodles from the sockets, only to be slurped up into the siren's blood-soaked maw. Growing tired of her flailing, bloody captive, María tore out his throat, arterial spray coating her enraged face. She gulped down his lifeblood before casting him aside, sending his body to Poseidon and his soul to Hades. Still not satisfied, she threw back her head and screamed, blood glistening on her coated scales like rubies.

Amidst a sea of red, Ioanna continued her bloody task. Both of her feet now resembled María's fins, and she gritted her teeth through the most excruciating process yet. Inserting the knife into her most private region, she sliced to the left. A scream escaped her lips as she quickly bit down on her blanket. The knife felt slippery in her blood-soaked hands, but she continued, flaying herself down her thighs all the way to her ankles. She felt as if the very fires of the great river Phlegethon flowed through her veins. But still, she persisted. *These men must pay*, she thought as she began to slice her other side. *They must pay for their transgressions. They go port to port, taking what they want, not caring who they hurt. They rape and cheat and steal and lie. They galavant off into the sunset, adhering to no moral code. They murdered my love, only for the crime that we are two women. THEY WILL PAY!* Ioanna threw back her head and howled with unadulterated rage as Terpsichore blessed her.

Her ragged flesh seared together, the pain reaching unprecedented thresholds as her legs fused into a tail. Her nails pierced out of her fingertips, elongating into razor-sharp talons. Her skin began to itch, her new talons tearing her skin to ribbons as rivulets of blood flowed from the newly opened wounds. Her jaw opened wide as her teeth were forced from their sockets, falling in a heap as they were replaced by obsidian fangs. Her rent flesh continued to shed, revealing sparkling scales underneath. The pain escalated as her eyes began to bulge, rolling back into her head as more vital fluid streamed down her face. The pain reached a climax before ultimately giving way to euphoric relief as Ioanna became reborn as a daughter of Terpsichore.

Alerted by her screams, an unsuspecting crew member flung the cabin door open. Before he could take in the bloody scene before him, Ioanna flicked her new claws, severing his head from his body. She opened her mouth, lasciviously lapping his essence as it pooled on the floor. Not satisfied with the blood of just one man, Ioanna began to use her powerful arms to propel her forward. She heard a fleshy *THUNK* above her, followed by screams. During the course of Ioanna's transformation, María made her way on board.

The sirens nodded, acknowledging one another before unleashing a reign of terror upon the crew. From across the deck, they both began to sing. Their otherworldly voices enraptured the men, luring them toward the sides of the ship. One by one, the men moved forward, nothing more than possessed thralls. As they reached the edge, claws flashed, simultaneously disemboweling them and slashing their throats. Blood and viscera coated the deck and its railings, creating tendrils down to the ocean where Poseidon and Hades gleefully awaited their new bodies and souls. The women let these men off easily. They were onlookers to their plight, guilty by association and in their silence. Finally, only two men remained alive. Frozen in terror as they saw the women's true forms, the Captain and his first mate began to tremble.

In a desperate attempt to save himself, the first mate prostrated himself before the women. "Please, we mean ye no harm. We be sorry 'or our sins. Please, 'ave mercy on us ol' men."

"Mercy? Mercy? How dare you?" María barked out a harsh laugh, causing the first mate to reel back as if he had been struck. "Where was your precious mercy when you grabbed us from our bed? When you made a spectacle of us before the very crew that just went to meet the gods? Where was your mercy when you threw me overboard to my death?" The first mate began to rise up, fury flashing in his eyes as he pulled out a hidden blade.

"Ye be jus' a woman af'r all. I'll be teach'n ye yer place now." He advanced upon María, who simply stared at him unflinchingly.

"Pathetic mortal, you cannot harm me," she cooed, advancing while beginning to sing again. The lilt of her voice mesmerized him as she pulled him into a carnal embrace. She kissed him as she sensually peeled down his pants. His lackluster erection hung between them as she cupped his buttocks. He leaned in for another kiss, just as her talons pierced his sacred hole, ripping it wide. Blood and shit splattered the floor as her claws worked, disemboweling the man from his asshole. He opened his mouth to scream, María's fangs sundered his tongue from his mouth. His eyes went wide as he took in her blood-soaked appearance, the blood of the crew coating her scales in an intoxicating array of glistening reds. From behind, Ioanna plunged her talons into the weathered skin of his back, slicing through skin and muscle while crushing several of his vertebrae. Finally, she felt her hand wrap around the prize. She grasped his heart and squeezed before ultimately tearing it from his limp form, the women leaving him dead in a pile of his own rancid filth. Together, they turned to face the captain.

The man fell to the ground, soaked in his own urine as he shook in absolute fear. He intended to beg for mercy, but horror stilled the words in his throat. "Father," spat Ioanna, "long have women been abused on your watch. No more I say." With a sneer mimicking her father, she removed his right hand. He used it repeatedly to abuse women, beating them and forcibly taking them against their will. Motioning for María to follow, Ioanna grabbed her father and pulled him to the mast. Together, they lashed him to the pole with the shit-covered intestines of his first mate. Ioanna disappeared for a moment as María licked her blood-covered lips. Ioanna quickly reappeared with a needle and thread. Eyeing her father, she promptly removed his withered manhood and pressed it to his lips. "As I've heard you tell countless women, choke on this." His eyes widened as she shoved the organ inside his mouth and forced his jaw shut. Then she began to sew. He struggled to no avail from their combined strength as María held his mouth and Ioanna sewed. María prized his eyes from their sockets, saving one for herself but sharing the other with Ioanna. They savored the delicious orbs and the bloody nerve endings before pausing to take a look at their handiwork.

Other than the mauled man before them, not a single human soul remained alive on the ship. The midday sun shone down, reflecting off the various pools of blood and viscera scattered around the deck. "This is your legacy, father. I hope you are proud," Ioanna spat. The ship would float forever, a bloody tribute to her father's cruelty and the vengeance of exploited women. Taking María's hand in hers, the two women dove into the sea, down to the depths, where their mother, Terpsichore, Queen of the Sirens, awaited them.

CRAB SALAD

BY DEREK THOMAS

Joey awoke and felt the warm, grainy sand of the Mexican beach underneath his back and in his butt crack. He was naked and his head was pounding. The heat of the blazing morning sun, already high in the sky, seared his tender, reddened skin. Afraid to open his eyes, he lay in repose, attempting to put together the pieces of what had happened the night before. As he listened to the waves slowly roll onto the beach, the events of the evening prior returned to his memory.

He and the boys had started their night at Senor Frog's, having appetizers and Coronas as a warmup for what would turn out to be an epic night. Joey, Brad and Gonzo stood to leave when Gabrielle approached their table. While speaking in Spanish directly to Joey, she placed her hand on his shoulder and softly pushed him back into his chair. Joey didn't understand a word she said, but was mesmerized by her beauty. She stood 5ft 8in tall in her heels. Her thick, lustrous hair was blacker than deep space and poured over her shoulders.

Her cinnamon-toned skin was flawless, marked only by a large turquoise tattoo of a crab that appeared to cover her entire chest. When she spoke, she spoke directly to Joey. He was entranced by the hunger in her almond-shaped jade eyes.

Neither Joey nor Brad spoke Spanish, however, Gonzo understood enough to get the gist of her words. She wanted them to join her friends for the night. Something about dancing Gonzo had thought. Joey nodded at Gabrielle, confirming his interest, knowing he would follow her anywhere. Her full lips parted with a smile as she offered her hand and led him, and his friends, into the night.

They took a taxi to Marina Albatros, where her friends waited on a forty-foot-long Catamaran named La Serina Perdida. Joey had thought they were going to a club, but this was cool too. As long as Gabrielle was there, he didn't care what they did. They were handed the first of many tequila slammers they would throw back during the night.

The recall of tequila, *so damn much tequila*, last night made Joey nauseous and saliva filled his mouth. He rolled onto all fours just before the sick erupted from his mouth. He puked until empty, then crawled to the water. He lay back down in the shallow surf, cooling his vulnerable skin.

His mind wandered back to the mysterious woman from last night. The skin-tight fabric of her yellow dress had barely restrained her firm, round ass, and perfect breasts. The tattoo drew him to her with a palpable tug, as if it were a sentient force.

Including Joey and his friends, there were eleven people on the boat as it disembarked for Isla Mujeres, a small, quaint island off the coast of Cancun. *Isla Mujeres? That must be where I am.*

Joey didn't want to face the day. He was too hungover and too weak. He continued to tap his mind for what had happened last night. He and Gabrielle drank and danced, drank and ground their hips, practically dry humping in front of everyone. Brad was hitting on a guy they called "Horse", for obvious reasons, and Gonzo spent the entire trip vomiting over the side into the sea.

When they arrived at the island, the captain turned on the lights under the boat, illuminating the crystal clear waters. Gabrielle immediately took off her dress and jumped into the cool ocean. The enraptured Joey followed her without hesitation. They entwined, they kissed, they consumed one another. The couple found their way to the shore where they made love—no; they had fucked. She had taken him in her mouth, her gorgeous green eyes staring at him the entire time. She had given him almost no time to recover, mounting and riding him aggressively. He moaned and thrust his hips up higher than he thought possible as she rode him to orgasm after screaming orgasm. Eventually, they passed out in each other's arms on this very beach.

Joey laid upon the beach smiling. Once again, his cock was as hard as steel.

But sometime during the night, she had left him. Left him here alone and naked on the beach. He sat up and opened his eyes. Squinting, he looked toward the ocean, expecting to see the boat there. Instead, he saw nothing but the open sea and the sun's blinding reflection on the water.

That was when reality slapped him in the face, and the panic took over. He jumped up and ran into the water up to his waist. He shouted her name several times, "Gabrielle! Gabrielle!". He looked in every direction. He saw no sign of civilization at all. Gabrielle, his friends, the boat, his clothes, his phone, and his wallet were all gone. They didn't exist in this new found world.

Joey stood and walked back toward the shoreline when he suddenly had a sharp and excruciating pain in the arch of his left foot. He yelled "SHIT!" as he fell forward and landed on all fours in the ankle deep water, as he saw an animal swim away with the receding water. At first, he thought it was a small shark, but as he rolled onto his butt and raised his foot out of the water, he saw part of the stingray's tail protruding from a jagged, circular hole. Blood poured from the wound. The pain was pure agony as he began to scream.

He calmed, eventually, and knew what he had to do. He grabbed the stinger, cutting his fingers as he took hold and yanked hard. The barbed tail ripped out a large mass of his flesh, and blood spurted into the air and painted the sand a deep crimson, only to be washed away as the next wave rolled onto the beach. Joey let out a manic scream. A waterfall of tears gushed down his face. He looked down at his foot, the wound now a gaping, bleeding laceration. He passed out in the rhythmic waves.

Joey opened his eyes. He had no idea how long he had been out, but thankfully, he felt no pain in the injured foot. Lying on his back, his reality returned to him, and he began to cry. He noticed that his heart was racing. *Am I having a heart attack?* It felt like a jackhammer in his chest. His breath was shallow. *What is happening to me?*

When he sat up, he saw a new horror. Three blue crabs were eating from the now swollen, seeping gash in his foot. He tried to kick the crabs away, but his leg remained still. Joey screamed, leaned forward and slapped the crabs off his injured foot. He went to rise, but neither leg would move. The sting had paralyzed him from the waist down. He heard a clicking sound coming from his left. Turning toward the sound, he saw over twenty blue crabs marching toward him.

Panicked, he rolled on to his stomach and army-crawled with his arms toward the mangrove fifty feet away. His heart felt like it would burst through his chest, his breath ragged and shallow, as he dragged his sun-burned body across the scratchy sand. Tears, sweat, and snot fell from his head as he tried to out-crawl the crabs. But they were too fast. They rode on Joey's back and legs, pulling plugs of delicious meat with razor-sharp pincers. He still could not feel the claws digging into his legs, but the ones ripping into his back felt like scalpels slicing through him.

He flung himself over onto his back, throwing some of the crabs off and crushing the soft bodies of the ones underneath his torso. He rolled back to his stomach and finally pulled himself into the mangrove.

He got himself into a sitting position against a mass of thin tree trunks; his worthless, mutilated legs lay before him, causing him to cry once again. He sat and tried to catch his breath and prayed that someone, anyone, would come along and save him. He desperately needed water, but at least he was out of the sun. With his energy completely spent, and no crabs attacking him at the moment, he dozed off in the shade.

Joey awoke with a torturous squeal as a large crab, with a carapace nearly a foot wide, pulled violently on his dick, blood flowing freely from the wound. He smashed the crab with his fist and looked around for more of the carnivorous crustaceans.

His fate was staring directly at him. Black crab eyes were everywhere he looked. He was surrounded. As they began to click their claws together, he was reminded of maniacal laughter. Joey screamed as hundreds of blue crabs attacked. They were everywhere. There were so many he couldn't possibly fight them off. Then he saw Gabrielle. She slowly rose from the water and smiled seductively at him the entire time. She wasn't walking, though; it appeared she was gliding up and toward him, almost as if she floated. Once her entire naked form emerged from the water, Joey could see how she was traveling. She was on her knees, sitting on what had to be the largest blue crab in existence. The crab was at least eight feet in diameter. Gabrielle climbed off the arthropod and walked toward him. Even as the crabs tore chunks of flesh away, Joey was mesmerized by the sway of her hips and the large turquoise tattoo that adorned her body.

The creatures gouged his eyes and sliced his reddened flesh, pulling him apart bit by tiny bit. Within minutes, he was no longer visible under the writhing, crustaceous mass that consumed him.

His screams now silenced; the crabs feasted all day, grateful for the bounty provided them by their queen.

MADE YOU LOOK

BY KATE REEDWOOD

A musty scent filled Jackie's nose, urging her to focus. It reminded her of her grandparent's old cellar, but it was deeper and danker, clinging to the back of her throat. Her stomach clenched as she breathed in the scent. Something close to her was rotting. Had something died? The pungent odor screamed at her, warning her to keep away.

Run.

Hide.

Jackie banged against the hard wall at her back as she jerked awake and opened her eyes. Pain lanced through her head like a spike of agony, mirroring the shouts of protest coming from her bound wrists and ankles. She moaned, unable to breathe deeply or scream thanks to the gag covering her mouth.

Fuck.

Her heart hammered in her chest as she glanced around the dimly lit room. Where the hell was she? And what the hell had happened?

Last thing she remembered was locking up Cooper's Books for the night and leaving through the back door to head to her car in the alleyway. Her mind had been focused on getting home to Stevie, just like every Thursday when she worked the late shift and had to close. She'd unlocked her car door and bent down to pick up some loose change that must have fallen on the ground and then—

A reflection glinted in the dimness, catching her attention as her eyes adjusted to the thin lighting. Twin glints. They shifted and brightened, then dimmed completely, making her freeze momentarily as recognition dawned. It was eyes. Glasses covered eyes.

Someone was watching her.

They'd leaned forward, then receded back into the shadows.

Were they caught like her and tied up too?

Or was it the person who had done this to her? Watching her in the dark. Like some crazy fucked-up psychopath who wanted God knows what.

Oh fuck, oh fuck, oh fuck.

Every story Jackie had ever heard about women getting abducted flooded her mind as the twin glints appeared from the shadows again and the figure slowly rose.

She let out a muted scream and frantically pulled against the cords binding her.

He was not tied up. He was not caught like her. He was definitely a 'he' though by his stocky build. Somewhere above her on the wall, a basement window let in just enough daylight that she could make out his shape and the shapes of other things now. A table at the far end of the rectangular room. Shelves. Stacks of boxes. Wooden stairs on the opposite wall from her, beneath which he'd been sitting on a chair tucked in the shadows.

The stairs meant a way out.

But what the hell did that matter if she couldn't even stand? A dank chill seeped through the concrete floor and into her bones. The zip ties didn't give an inch to her struggles. The best she could do was wriggle on the hard floor like a worm in the sticky dirt that smelled like...dead things. She'd found a mouse once in a cupboard in her trailer when cleaning it out. It had been dead for probably a week, she'd guessed. Maybe it had eaten poison. Maybe it had been old, or something else had happened. Whatever the cause of its death, it had smelled exactly like this basement.

She wrinkled her nose, recoiling from the smell and the images of maggots that wriggled through her mind.

Don't think about it. Don't think.

Vomiting in the gag would not be good. She swallowed hard and tried to get hold of herself. But it was nearly impossible to think straight with how much her head pounded. Had she been hit? Drugged? What the fuck day was it even? How long had she been here? It was dark when she'd locked up the store, but faint light was coming through that window. Dawn or dusk?

Oh, Stevie...

The thought of her ten-year-old son sitting home alone and terrified out of his mind about why she'd not come back made her pull against the zip ties again despite the fresh red cuts they left on her wrists. She needed to get out of here. She'd always hated leaving her only child to mind himself after school for hours. But who could she trust? No family. No friends in this town. Where was her cell phone? He'd probably called her wondering where she was. Would he think to call the cops as well?

Goddammit. Tears stung her eyes as fear clashed with rage. She glared at the shadowy man standing there, watching her struggle against helplessness. How dare he do this to her? To her son. How dare the world be filled with predators feeding off the vulnerable? If she had a knife, she'd cut him and make him bleed for what he'd done.

But she didn't know if it had even been him who had taken her, now did she?

Calm down, Jackie. Be nice to whoever he is. There has to be a way out of this.

The figure took a step toward her and stopped. Then a moment later, she winced and blinked as the room suddenly changed from murky darkness to bright light. Stark shadows grew and shrank as the light wavered and swung back and forth, cast by a naked bulb attached to a cord hanging from the ceiling.

She stared at the man looming above her. Then a second later she realized her terrible mistake. She should have shut her eyes and kept them squeezed tight, no matter what he did. If he was her captor, there was no way he'd let her go now that she knew what he looked like and could describe him to the police. Average height and build. Grey coveralls. Greying brown hair. Flat grey eyes that stared at her from behind thin-rimmed spectacles. There was no spark of interest in his gaze or any hint of compassion or wariness. He stared down at her as if she was a bug he could squash with his foot if he wanted to—and she knew in that second that's exactly what she was. A bug. A thing. Not a person. Not a woman name Jackie Barber with a young child named Stephen. She was a problem he needed to take care of.

Her stomach clenched as the trembling started and spread through each of her limbs. But still, there had to be a way out of this. She didn't recognize him, but maybe if he removed the gag, she could talk to him. Get him to see she was a nice person just trying to live her life. She'd never harm a fly. She even caught spiders and let them go outside rather than kill them. No, no, she wasn't mean at all, which meant she deserved to live, right?

Except good people died every day, caught in the wrong place at the wrong time. Her heart sank as each second passed and the man didn't reach down to untie her or even offer a kind smile.

Please, God...

She tried not to think about what the rotting smell of meat likely meant. Or the news reports she'd half-listened to on the television about missing people in the community. The body that was found near a trail in the woods last week, limbs severed and head missing. That stuff happened to other people, not here, not now, not to her.

Not me. Please, God, not me.

The man's blank expression never changed as he put a hand into his coveralls pocket and pulled out something that jingled. It was the only sound she'd heard since the click of the lightbulb chain being pulled and her own choked whimpers.

As he bent down on one knee in front of her, she shook her head and pleaded at him with whimpers and her eyes.

No, no, no, please, not me. Let me go. I'll be good. I'll do whatever you want. Just please, please, please give me a chance.

If the man recognized her despair, he didn't show it. He chose a coin from the loose change clutched in his hand. The coin flashed in the light as he tossed it into the air, then caught it again. His gaze found hers briefly before he looked at the result. Was it heads or tails? Which would be better for her?

He looked at the coin. With his back to the light and his face in shadow, even his skin looked grey and his teeth like ash as his thin lips stretched into a rictus grin.

He held the coin out to her so she could see the result.

Heads.

Then, without saying a word, he stood and moved to the table at the far end of the room, which she could see was a workbench. Dark stains covered it, as did a variety of tools, including a saw and a large glass jar.

Oh shit, oh fuck, this can't be happening. This can't be real.

She thought of the coins she'd spied on the ground by her car door. The impulse to pick them up had been automatic. An afterthought while she'd focused on getting in the car and driving home. She hadn't paid attention at all to her surroundings other than those damn coins that had caught her eye.

What if he had placed the change by the car to trap her? Flipped a coin to see what would happen to her then, too? Heads—if she bent to pick the change up, he grabbed her. Tails—he would leave her alone?

Shit. Was all this madness because he made me look at some damn coins?

The sound of his cheery whistling while he tied on a plastic apron and readied his instruments was dulled by the discordant buzzing that filled Jackie's mind as she spied the shelf behind the table...and froze. Glass jars filled the shelves, each containing a human head, with eyes that glinted in the light. No, not eyes. Silver coins were wedged in the empty sockets surrounded by rubbery bloated flesh. The coins seemed to wink at her as the light caught them, while the heads slowly drifted in the fluid filled jars.

Heads. The coin toss had chosen heads.

And hers was next.

Despite the gag, Jackie screamed.

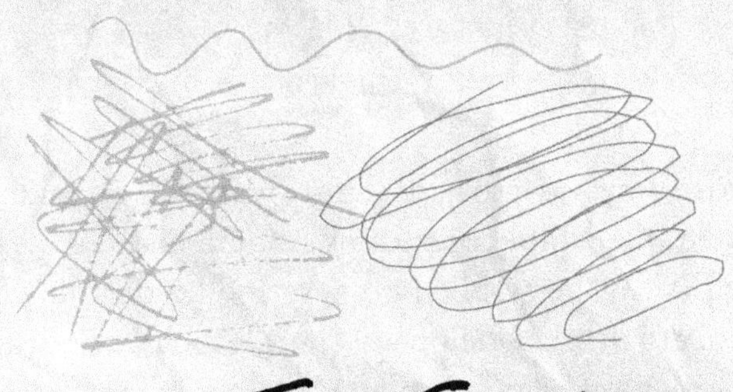

THE SHED

BY ANDY EDGE

W alter woke to the sound of rain tapping against his window. He lay there for a moment, staring at the ceiling, a familiar emptiness settling in his chest.

He dragged himself out of bed and shuffled to the bathroom. At six foot, he was average looking, brown hair, brown eyes, he had no remarkable features that stood out. Even so, he avoided looking in the mirror. He brushed his teeth and splashed water on his face. Back in his bedroom, he pulled on his barista uniform of a black polo shirt and jeans that had seen better days.

In the kitchen, he halfheartedly ate a bowl of cereal while checking his social media. His feed overflowed with smiling faces and exciting lives. All of it was so different from his own stagnant one. He checked the dating site only to find his last few messages to potential dates ignored. With a sigh, he slid his phone into his pocket.

He never understood what was wrong with him. Why did he get passed over on the dating sites? Why was it so hard for him to find friends? Why was it so hard at forty years old? Shouldn't he have figured these things out at this point in his life?

Dreading the day, he grabbed his keys and headed out the door. The walk to the coffee shop was short, a cool rain misting his face. He kept his head down, preparing himself for the long hours of fake smiles and mundane conversations ahead.

Walter pushed open the door, the bell chiming above him as he stepped inside. He shook the rain from his coat and ran a hand through his damp, thinning hair. The familiar rich aroma of coffee grounds and the hiss of the espresso machine greeted him.

"Morning, Walter," Mitch called from behind the counter, where he was setting out fresh pastries in the display case.

"Hey, Mitch." Walter hung his coat on the hook in the back and grabbed his apron. He suppressed a yawn as he tied the apron strings behind his back. The early mornings never seemed to get easier, even after years at this job. Walter took his place behind the register and began wiping down the counters until they gleamed under the soft lighting. Another dreary morning, another day going through the motions.

He glanced out the rain-streaked windows at the gray cityscape. People hurried by under colorful umbrellas, shoulders hunched against the wind. Walter wondered, not for the first time, what it would be like to be one of them. Heading to a job he found meaningful, maybe a family waiting at home. Instead, loneliness wrapped around him like a well-worn sweater.

The first few customers of the day trickled in, seeking shelter from the rain and their morning caffeine fix. Walter pasted on a smile as he took their orders, his "Good morning! What can I get for you?" rang out with forced cheer.

He reached to pour a cup of dark roast, and a sudden itch flared across his forearm. When he glanced down, he saw a small patch of red, irritated skin. He frowned and scratched at it absently before he finished the order.

The door chimed again, signaling the arrival of more damp, bleary-eyed customers. Walter pushed the itch from his mind as he threw himself into the rhythm of the morning rush. Cups clattered, milk steamed, and espresso flowed as he crafted drink after drink.

During the next few hours, the itch grew more insistent, prickling under his skin like a thousand tiny needles. During a brief lull, he rolled up his sleeve to investigate, and his eyes widened. The rash had spread, creeping from wrist to halfway up his forearm in ruddy, raised patches.

Walter swallowed hard. This was more than simple dry skin. An unsettling feeling lodged in his chest as he tugged his sleeve back down. Something was wrong, but he couldn't afford to dwell on it now. The line at the register only grew longer and the steam from the milk frother erased all thoughts of strange rashes.

The next time Walter had a break, he again pushed his sleeve up to get a better look at the rash. To his astonishment, the red, bumpy skin had spread even more. Now it was up past his elbow.

"Hey, Walter, can you grab more milk from the—whoa, what's up with your arm?" Mitch's question cut through Walter's thoughts.

Walter quickly tugged his sleeve down, but it was too late. Mitch had seen the rash.

"It's nothing," Walter said. "Just some dry skin."

Mitch raised an eyebrow. "That doesn't look like dry skin to me. It's all red and blotchy. Maybe you should get that checked out."

Walter felt a flare of irritation. He didn't need Mitch telling him what to do. He didn't need anyone prying into his business.

"It's fine. Don't worry about it."

Mitch held up his hands in surrender. "Alright, alright. But if it gets worse, promise me you'll get it looked at."

Walter nodded, eager to end the conversation. "Yeah, sure. I promise."

Mitch gave him a long, scrutinizing look before turning back to the espresso machine.

Walter glanced at the clock. His shift was almost over. He could feel the itch spreading, crawling up his arm like a living thing. Walter finished his work on autopilot, consumed with thoughts of the rash. What if Mitch was right? What if it was something serious?

Walter stepped into his small apartment, the door closing behind him with a soft click. He tossed his coat onto the floor near the door and ripped his shirt off over his head. He'd practically run home, so anxious was he to get a good look at his arm. He scratched at the inflamed skin. The itch was maddening, crawling and prickling beneath the surface. He realized the rash crept higher now, up his arm to his shoulder.

He craned his neck, trying to get a better look. His stomach dropped as he saw the rash had indeed spread, covering his entire upper arm and shoulder blade.

Seized by a gripping fear, Walter rushed to the bathroom. He flicked on the light and turned his back to the mirror, twisting to get a better look. The rash was everywhere, angry and red, covering his back in splotchy patches.

Panic rising in his throat, Walter yanked his shirt back on and grabbed his keys. He needed something to calm the itch, to stop the spread.

The walk to the drugstore passed in a haze. Walter stood in the aisle, staring blankly at the rows of anti-itch creams and ointments. He grabbed the first one he saw and hurried to the register, avoiding eye contact with the cashier as shame at the rash, something he couldn't even control, caused his anxiety to worsen.

Back in his apartment, Walter unscrewed the cap of the cream and began applying it liberally everywhere he could reach. He sighed as the cool ointment soothed his burning skin. He slathered it on his arm, his shoulder and his back.

Exhausted, Walter collapsed onto his couch and reached for his laptop. He spent the next few hours scouring the internet, typing "red itchy rash" into the search bar over and over.

The results ranged from mildly concerning to downright terrifying. Allergic reactions, autoimmune disorders, rare skin conditions. Each new page sent a fresh wave of anxiety crashing over him.

As the night progressed, Walter's eyelids drooped, and he succumbed to the weight of exhaustion. The once-sharp images on his laptop screen blurred into an indistinct jumble of words. With a weary sigh, he gently closed the computer, placing it beside him on the couch. Leaning back against the plush cushions, Walter allowed himself to sink into their comforting embrace and he drifted off into a restless slumber.

The shrill beep of Walter's phone alarm jolted him awake. He groaned, his body stiff from sleeping on the couch. He stumbled to the bathroom, his mind still foggy as he turned the shower on, letting steam fill the small space.

Eyes half-closed, Walter stepped into the shower and reached for the soap. He barely touched his arm when a sharp pain jolted him fully awake.

The rash, which had been merely itchy and inflamed the night before, had become disgusting, oozing blisters. They were a horrid yellow color, some of them weeping fluid.

Walter's stomach turned. Bile rose in his throat. His pulse pounded in his ears as he realized the rash had spread even further, now creeping across his chest toward his other arm and over half his stomach.

He finished his shower in record time, barely able to stand the feeling of the water on his blistered skin. He stepped out, toweling off gingerly, and reached for the anti-itch cream.

Walter slathered the ointment over the rash and blisters, his fingers trembling. The blisters made the application painful, and he gritted his teeth. Trepidation gnawed at his insides as he carefully pulled on his shirt, his movements slow and deliberate. The material chafed the sensitive blisters all over his body. Each cautious gesture elicited a wince of pain.

During the commute to the coffee shop, Walter tried to make sense of what was happening to him. This was more than a simple rash. This was something serious. Was he going to die?

He pushed through the door of the shop, the familiar chime of the bell doing little to calm his nerves. He went through the motions of his opening duties, his body on autopilot. At the sink, as he washed his hands, Mitch caught sight of the rash. His eyes widened, his brow furrowing with concern. "Jesus, Walter! That looks terrible. You need to see a doctor, man."

Walter bristled, his fear manifesting into anger. "I told you, Mitch, it's no big deal. I'm handling it."

Mitch shook his head. "That's not something you can just handle on your own. Those blisters look infected. You need medical attention."

Walter pushed the faucet off, water droplets flying. "I said I'm fine. Just drop it and get back to work."

He stormed away from the sink, leaving a bewildered and worried Mitch in his wake. Walter's head throbbed as he took his place behind the counter. He could feel the rash burning beneath his clothes, the blisters spreading everywhere.

A few days later, Walter sat in the cramped waiting room of the clinic, his leg bouncing nervously. He had finally caved, taking time off work to seek medical attention for the rash that had overtaken his body.

He shifted uncomfortably in the plastic chair. Every movement he made hurt. Wearing clothes had become agonizing. The rash continued to spread over the last few days. It had moved down his body, over his thighs, and even his most sensitive parts. Not only that, now you could see the horrible rash and blisters on his neck, which made it impossible for him to hide.

"Walter?" a nurse called, poking her head out from behind a door. Mustering his courage, Walter stood and entered the examination room on her heels, his unease obvious.

The doctor, a middle-aged man with a receding hairline and a tired expression, barely glanced up from his clipboard as Walter entered.

"What seems to be the problem?" he asked without preamble.

Walter hesitated, suddenly feeling foolish. "I have this rash," he began nervously. "It started small, but it's spread all over my body. It's painful and itchy, and I don't know what to do."

The doctor sighed, setting down his clipboard. "Let's take a look."

Walter gingerly removed his shirt. The doctor didn't even blink as he looked at it with disinterest. He prodded at a patch on Walter's shoulder, making him wince. "How long has this been going on?" the doctor asked.

"A few weeks," Walter replied. "It started small, but it's just gotten worse and worse."

The doctor hummed thoughtfully. He stepped back, crossing his arms over his chest. "Walter, I think this might be a case of psychosomatic dermatitis."

Walter blinked, confused. "Psycho...what?"

"Psychosomatic dermatitis," the doctor repeated. "It's a condition where psychological factors, like stress or anxiety, manifest as physical symptoms, like a rash."

Walter shook his head. "But this isn't just in my head. The rash is real. It's painful."

The doctor shrugged. "The mind is a powerful thing. It can make the body believe it's experiencing things that aren't really there."

He scribbled something on his clipboard and tore off a sheet of paper, handing it to Walter. "I'm prescribing you a mild anti-anxiety medication. I think if you can reduce your stress, the rash will clear up on its own. You don't see anyone else walking around like this, do you? It's not normal. So get yourself under control."

Walter stared at the prescription in his hand, a mix of disbelief and frustration welling up inside him. This wasn't all in his head. The rash was real. It wasn't some figment of his imagination.

But the doctor was already ushering him out of the room, on to the next patient. Walter dressed quickly, the prescription crumpling in his fist.

He left the clinic feeling worse than when he had arrived. The doctor's words echoed around him, "it's all in your head." But Walter knew better. He knew that whatever was happening to him was real. He tossed the prescription in the trash when he entered his apartment. Walter sank onto his couch, his head in his hands. Once more, he was on his own.

Walter stood behind the counter at work a few weeks later, his skin burning and itching beneath the layers of clothing he wore to conceal the rash. He tried to focus on his work, on the familiar routine of taking orders and making drinks. But the pain grew worse every day. He didn't know what to do.

As he rang up a customer's order, Walter's sleeve rode up slightly, exposing a patch of blistered, reddened skin on his wrist. He quickly tugged it back down, but not before the customer, a young woman with a child beside her, caught sight of it.

Her gaze darted to Walter's wrist, and her eyes widened with a mixture of fear and concern. "Is that contagious?" she questioned, gesturing towards the source of her apprehension.

Walter forced a smile, trying to project a calmness he didn't feel. "No, no, it's not contagious," he assured her. "Just a bit of eczema. Nothing to worry about."

But the woman didn't look convinced. She pulled her child closer, turning the little one's face away from Walter. "Don't look, sweetie," she said. "Let's go."

She abandoned her order and hurried out of the shop, leaving Walter to watch her hasty departure. A crushing sense of rejection and hopelessness descended upon him, causing his shoulders to droop under the burden of his sorrows. She hadn't bothered to ask how he was coping or if he needed support; her sole concern was whether his condition might somehow impact her. In that instant, Walter was engulfed by an overwhelming feeling of isolation, realizing that he was utterly alone in his struggle. He was grateful that Mitch, busy with the espresso machine, hadn't noticed the interaction.

Walter absently reached up to adjust his collar, his fingers brushing against the rough, blistered skin that now crept up his neck and over one ear. He winced at the contact, a fresh wave of pain radiating from the affected area. The rash was impossible to hide now, a repulsive mask slowly overtaking his features.

Walter swallowed hard. He couldn't go on like this, couldn't keep pretending that everything was normal. But what choice did he have? So he pushed through the pain, through the stares and the whispers. He focused on the rhythm of the work, on the familiar motions of making coffee and ringing up orders.

Halfway through his shift, he stepped over toward the employee restroom. He could barely focus on anything but the incessant, maddening itch that tormented every inch of his skin. As he reached for the restroom door, Mitch's voice stopped him. "Hey, Walter, where are you going?"

Walter turned, his hand still on the door handle. "To the restroom. Why?"

Mitch shifted uncomfortably, his eyes darting to the patches of blistered skin visible above Walter's collar. "Listen, man, I've been thinking. Maybe you shouldn't use the employee restroom anymore."

Walter blinked, confusion and hurt welling up inside him. "What? Why not?"

Mitch sighed, rubbing the back of his neck. "It's just...until you get whatever is going on with you fixed, it might be better if you used the public restroom instead."

Walter stared at him, a mix of disbelief and anger churning in his gut. "Are you serious? You're banning me from the employee restroom?"

Mitch held up his hands, a placating gesture. "It's not a ban, Walter. It's just a precaution. We don't know what's wrong with you, and we can't risk spreading it to the other employees. It's not normal."

Walter struggled to contain his growing frustration, his entire body tensing as he fought the urge to lash out. He wanted to argue, to shout that he wasn't contagious, that he wasn't a risk to anyone. But the words stuck in his throat, choked by the lump of emotion that had risen there.

Instead, he turned on his heel and stalked away, making the long trek to the public restroom at the front of the shop. With every step, he could feel the eyes of the customers on him, could hear their whispers and gasps as they caught sight of his afflicted skin.

"Mommy, what's wrong with that man's face?" a child asked loudly, pointing at Walter.

"Don't stare, honey," the mother chided, pulling the child away. But her eyes, wide with disgust and fear, never left Walter.

He hurried past them, his head down, his cheeks burning with humiliation. Their stares were daggers in his back, their muffled laughter and exclamations of revulsion chased him into the restroom. He locked himself in a stall and leaned against the door as he tried to regain his composure.

But the damage was done. Walter felt like a pariah, a monster to be gawked at and shunned. He looked down at his hands, at the blisters and lesions that covered them. What was wrong with him? He felt like a stranger in his own skin, a freak to be hidden away from the world.

Walter jolted upright, sleep suddenly banished as his skin erupted with the all-too-familiar, overwhelming sensation that had become his ceaseless companion, making every nerve ending scream for relief. He lay in bed, dreading the moment he would have to move and face another day of stares, whispers, and isolation.

As he shifted, trying to find a comfortable position, his arm brushed against the rough fabric of his sheets. A new sharp pain flared, more intense than anything he'd felt before. Without thinking, Walter scratched at it vigorously, his nails digging into the blistered, inflamed skin.

And then, to his utter shock and horror, a sizable chunk of skin peeled right off into his hand.

Walter bolted upright, adrenaline surging through his veins. His eyes widened in disbelief at the sight of the area where the blisters had once marred his skin. The flesh was sloughing off, not in the delicate flakes he had grown accustomed to, but in alarming, sizable patches that revealed new, raw skin beneath. His body had begun to shed its damaged outer layer.

With trembling fingers, Walter grasped another edge of the loose skin and pulled. It came away, revealing another layer beneath. Walter's breath came in short, sharp gasps of pain as he continued to peel away the layers of dead, blistered skin. It was like unwrapping a macabre gift, never knowing what waited beneath each layer.

With each layer stripped away, Walter delved deeper into the unknown. His fingers trembled as they brushed against a surface entirely foreign to him. Gone was the soft, flaky texture of skin; in its place was something hard, smooth, and cool to the touch. He hesitated and then peeled away the last layer of dead skin.

In place of the expected raw, tender flesh lay a new type of skin altogether–hard, almost metallic in texture, and shimmering with an iridescent, brilliant blue hue. The surface glimmered in the light. It was beautiful. And unlike anything Walter had ever seen before.

The blue skin covered his entire forearm, from wrist to elbow. It was smooth and flawless, the color shifting and changing as it caught the light. Walter ran his fingers over it, marveling at the alien feel of it, the way it seemed to hum with a strange inner energy.

Questions raced through his mind, each more terrifying than the last. What was happening to him? What did this strange cobalt skin mean? Was he even human anymore, or was he becoming something else entirely?

After calling off work, Walter stood in front of the bathroom mirror. Fear and anticipation coursed through him. With trembling hands, he peeled away the layers of dead, blistered skin. It was an agonizing process. Each tug and pull sent shockwaves of pain through his body. The skin clung to him stubbornly, as if reluctant to reveal the truth beneath.

Hours turned into days as Walter methodically worked to remove the old, decaying layers. He would peel until his fingers were raw and his body slick with sweat and tears. The pain was overwhelming, driving him to the brink of despair.

He had to take frequent breaks, collapsing onto the bathroom floor in exhaustion. The cool tiles provided a break against his feverish, oversensitive skin. In those moments, he questioned whether he could go on, whether the agony was worth the revelation.

But each time, as he caught sight of the brilliant, iridescent blue emerging beneath the dead skin, Walter found the strength to continue. It was a slow, excruciating unveiling of each new patch of cobalt skin.

As the days wore on, the changes accelerated. When Walter peeled the skin from his scalp, his hair came out in clumps, littering the floor in lifeless tangles. But in its place, fresh growth emerged. Thick, lustrous strands of a brilliant white, a beautiful contrast to the deep blue of his skin.

The transformation was all-consuming, reshaping every part of him. His nails, once cracked and yellowed, fell away to reveal smooth, opalescent talons. His eyes, bloodshot and watery from the constant pain, gradually cleared to a piercing silver.

By the end of the week, Walter was utterly unrecognizable. He stood before the mirror, his old skin lying in desiccated piles around him, and marveled at the being he had become. The pain, the suffering, had been almost unbearable. But the result was breathtaking.

As Walter moved, the iridescent blue of his newfound skin shimmered and shifted, catching the light in mesmerizing ways. The smooth, cool surface of this alien layer seemed to imbue his every motion with a powerful, almost supernatural grace, transforming his once-ordinary movements into something ethereal and captivating. His white hair, now full and flowing, framed his face like a halo. Even his posture had changed, his spine straightening as if freed from an unseen weight.

Walter took a deep, shuddering breath, the first painless inhale in what felt like an eternity. The agony of the transformation was fading, replaced by a growing sense of strength.

Walter stepped out into the world, a profound transformation having taken hold of his entire being. The physical changes were undeniable, but the internal shift left him breathless.

For the first time in his existence, a radiance emanated not just from his altered appearance, but from the very core of his soul. This metamorphosis had not only reshaped his outer form, but had also ignited a long-dormant spark within him, awakening a powerful self-assurance and a belief in his own worth. With each step, Walter embraced his new confidence, ready to face the world as a man reborn, forever changed by the extraordinary journey he had undergone.

The stares and whispers that had once haunted him now bounced off his iridescent skin like harmless raindrops. He held his head high, his silver eyes gleaming, knowing that he was worthy of a better life—a life filled with joy and fulfillment. He wasn't normal, but he didn't care anymore. What even did *normal* mean, anyway?

In a moment of clarity, Walter realized the coffee shop, with its daily drudgery and petty dramas, no longer held a place in his new existence. He quit without hesitation.

Instead, Walter found himself drawn to a quiet little bookstore nestled between two towering office buildings. The moment he stepped inside, he felt a sense of belonging, the musty scent of books and the soft rustle of pages a balm to his soul.

The owner, a kind-eyed elderly woman, took one look at Walter and smiled. She saw beyond his striking appearance, recognizing the gentle, intelligent spirit within. When Walter inquired about a job opening, she hired him on the spot, her instincts telling her that this extraordinary being would bring a special magic to her shop.

Walter settled into his new role and found the peace and contentment that had always eluded him. He moved through the stacks with a quiet reverence, his cobalt hands lovingly caressing the spines of the books. He shared his passion with customers, his confidence and charm drawing people to him like moths to a flame.

One afternoon, as Walter arranged a display of new arrivals, a familiar voice jolted him from his thoughts. He turned to see Mitch, his former coworker, standing before him, his mouth agape and his eyes wide with astonishment.

"Walter?" Mitch said in disbelief. "Is that really you?"

Walter smiled, a dazzling display of white teeth against his blue skin. "In the flesh!"

Mitch shook his head, struggling to reconcile the stunning, self-assured being before him with the shy, withdrawn man he had once known. "You look incredible," he managed. "What happened to you?"

Walter's smile softened, a hint of mystery playing at the corners of his lips. "Let's just say I've shed my old skin," he said. "And found something far more precious beneath."

Walter sat in his living room, the soft glow of his laptop screen illuminating his iridescent features. It had been a long day at the bookstore, but a fulfilling one. He had lost himself in the pages of countless stories, sharing his love of literature with eager customers.

But now, in the quiet of his apartment, Walter felt a different excitement stir within him. He had spent so many years hiding from the world, shying away from the possibility of connection and intimacy. But with his transformation had come a desire to embrace all that life had to offer.

With a deep breath, Walter navigated to the familiar dating site, the one where he had experienced so much rejection and disappointment in the past. But this time, he uploaded a new profile picture. A stunning selfie showcasing his cobalt skin, white hair, and silver eyes.

The photo captured his essence perfectly, the joy and self-assurance that now radiated from every pore. It was a far cry from the old, grainy pictures he had once used, the ones that seemed to apologize for his very existence.

Not long after posting the updated photo, a notification alert disrupted the silence. Walter's fingers trembled slightly as he opened the message, his anticipation building with each passing moment. As his eyes scanned the words on the screen, a wave of excitement washed over him.

"Hey there," the message began, "I love your look! I'd love to get to know the person behind those stunning silver eyes. What do you say we grab a coffee sometime soon?"

Walter leaned back in his chair, a smile spreading across his face. The message, so simple and straightforward, felt like a validation of everything he had gone through, all the pain and suffering he had endured to become his true self.

He thought back to the long, agonizing days of his transformation, the searing pain as he shed his old skin layer by layer. He remembered the moments of doubt, fearing he would never emerge from his chrysalis, believing he would be trapped in a state of endless suffering.

But now, as he sat there, his fingertips poised over the keyboard to craft a response, Walter knew every moment had been worth it. The pain, the isolation, the self-doubt, all of it were necessary steps on the path to these moments.

With a grin, Walter typed out his reply, his fingers flying over the keys. "I would love to," he wrote. "I know a great little coffee shop, one where the baristas know how to make a mean latte. How about tomorrow afternoon?"

He hit send, a giddy excitement bubbling up within him. For the first time in his life, Walter felt truly seen. He had finally become precisely who he was always meant to be.

Apologetic Anna

by Kristal Shanahan

Dusk approached and Abby focused on swimming near the dock, oblivious to the upcoming nightfall and the dangers surrounding it. The humidity was suffocating, making the swim more necessity than pleasure. Crickets chirped and cicadas could be heard at a deafening level, unaware of the looming depravity. Abby loved to swim at night to clear her head. Tonight was no different. Normally Levi would join her, but he had to finish a few things at his parent's house; he had to skip the swim with Abby, promising to join her later.

Spring Break was nearly over as her thoughts kept wandering back to Levi currently at his nearby lake house. Every spring and summer, she looked forward to the two weeks out of the year they spent together. Their parents went to college together and remained the best of friends all these years later. Yesterday she saw Levi for the first time in a new way, and those intrusive thoughts were welcomed with a sigh of longing.

She thought about him nearly every waking moment and had such high hopes for more than a great friendship.

As Abby pulled herself up from the water onto the rotted, wooden section of the dock, she noticed something glimmering from the sun's reflection at the edge of the woods. Toweling off and laying her beach towel by the firepit that was blazing, she sauntered over to get a closer look. Walking on the worn path to where the buried item lay beneath leaves and brush, she hesitated to pick it up. Old and battered, the doll caked with grime and wearing a tattered dress gave clues to being lost for decades. Deciding to throw caution to the wind, she wiped off as much dirt and leaves from it that would fall away using her bare hands. She carried it back to the dock and set it down on one of the Adirondack chairs as she draped the towel around her shoulders and tempered the fire. She looked at the tag on the inside of the doll's dress. The name "Anna" was clearly scribbled in faded ink.

Abby sat down and grabbed a beer from the ice chest. She looked at the beer she accidentally picked up. Stella wouldn't do. That was for Levi. She wrinkled her nose and put back the beer, digging for something better. Finding a few mini bottles of Skrewball, she sat back, satisfied with her choice.

Stella tastes like piss. I don't understand why Levi loves it, she thought.

While waiting on Levi to arrive, she chugged the first bottle and started her second as she daydreamed of what she hoped would happen between them. Interrupted by someone yelling her name, she snapped out of it. Branches cracking and heavy footfalls could be heard behind her. Turning around, she saw Levi with his sexy lopsided grin.

"Abby! There you are. I've been looking for you." Levi walked up, grabbed a beer and sat in the chair next to her.

Holding her gaze, he asked, "What the hell is that in the other chair?" Pointing towards the doll, he chugged his Stella and waited for an answer.

"Excuse me, sir, it's a vintage doll that I dragged over here from the woods." Spoken in her most fake, snobbish tone, she glanced over at him and gave him the most flirtatious smile she could manage.

"We had plans to meet here. Did you forget, or did you have more chores at home to do?" Abby asked.

She knew he could see her dock from his lake house. They were actually neighbors. Abby studied him like a textbook. Lost in thought again, she didn't see Levi stand up and move toward her, setting his beer bottle down. He stood before her with eyes that screamed with desire. He gently grabbed her hands, encouraging her to stand up. They stood facing each other at a comfortable, close distance.

"Abby, I have to be honest with you. This trip, um, I looked forward to seeing you more than ever before. I really care about you. We've known each other for so long and have been great friends. I want to be more, but I need to know what you are feeling? I don't want to be wrong about this. That would be awkward." He laughed nervously.

Abby looked at Levi and melted. She moved her body closer to his, and there was no air able to escape between them. Abby was still in her bikini from her swim earlier, but the heat was not only rising from the fire pit, but deep within her. Levi's desire was apparent as he gently kissed her mouth slowly, skimmed her breasts, and he gave her bottom a light squeeze. He broke their passionate embrace to throw her towel down on the dock by the fire and they kissed again, but with more force and aggression. Abby untied her bikini top, and it fell to the side of her. Levi, with care, removed the other half of her bikini and tossed it behind him. While frantically kissing and their hands explored each other, they laid down after Levi lost all his clothes with Abby's assistance. He kissed a trail down her body, beginning with her neck, and progressed to her firm breasts.

He glanced up at her to see if she was enjoying herself. She was softly moaning with her eyes closed, so he kept going. When he reached her thighs, he continued to kiss her, caressing her, and moving in between her legs. Her hands ran through his thick locks of hair and then firmly gripped the towel. Levi never enjoyed sex more than he did at that moment, kissing and running his tongue between her legs until she bucked under him and called out his name. He then entered her and they moved together like they had been fucking for years. The next half hour was pure bliss for the both of them. Afterwards, the comfortable silence between them felt natural as they held each other tight with lingering, light caresses.

They began to hungrily kiss and caress each other again, but they knew they would have to get dressed soon, as their parents would be home anytime. Their parents were close friends and went out for drinks. A local bar, *Sutures,* is where the two families spent much of their time. Being in their twenties now, it wouldn't be the end of the world if their parents caught them together, but it wouldn't be ideal either.

"Levi, does this mean we're dating?" Giggling, she gazed into his eyes, but was nervous about his answer. She brushed her chestnut hair away from her perfectly shaped lips. Her head was buzzing with excitement and bourbon, thinking of the possibilities and also self doubt was creeping in as it often does.

"Abby, I would love nothing more than to be exclusive. We graduate from college soon and we wouldn't have to date long distance, maybe for two to three months? We've known each other for years. I love you, and there isn't anyone I would ever want in this world but you."

Continuing to lie next to each other, each lost in thought for a few moments, the sounds of nature were enveloped in a sudden silence. Nocturnal elements ceased to exist.

"Levi, I, I don't know what to say. Well, yes, I do. I have always loved you. I mean, before, it was as a friend, but now it's definitely more. Not just because you satisfied me like I really didn't think was possible. Lord, that is cheesy as hell, but true." She laughed and looked at Levi.

"Then we agree. Let's get dressed, and we can tell our parents the great news. They will be so excited to hear this. Let me grab your bottoms." Levi gave her a sly smile.

He reached over to grab her bikini bottoms when he heard a small childlike voice behind him. He quickly swiveled as a small hand reached out, touching his and holding Abby's bikini.

"Hi, I'm Anna. Who are you guys? Thanks for saving me from drowning in the mud and branches! Oh, here's your clothes...um you two might want to get dressed pretty quickly." Her voice and tone mimicked Abby's to a tea. As she handed Abby's bikini bottoms to Levi, he quickly grabbed them as his eyes widened at the disbelief of what he was seeing, and the hair on his arms stood at attention.

"Fuck! What the hell?" Levi pulled his hand away and saw that there was a thin, jagged gash with blood pooling at his feet. He grabbed his shirt after he put his swim trunks back on to stop the bleeding.

"Oh, no. I did it again. I'm so sorry. I try so hard to be good, but I just...can't," Anna spoke softly.

She hobbled slowly toward Abby. Blonde, dirty hair partially covered her eyes, which moved rapidly back and forth with a quiet clicking.

"My God, what are you? You look like a ventriloquist doll that crawled from Hell." Abby spoke with trepidation and fear melting into sheer horror.

"Goodness no, Abby." Laughing, she crept even closer to Abby.

"I have a passive aggressive personality, but I haven't been to hell yet." With a permanent plastic smile plastered across her face, Anna laughed again. "You are so funny, Abby! I like you, but stop backing away from me. I want to *play*. My brother over there wants to play too. He's not as nice as I am, though."

Looking toward the wooded area in the recesses of the trees, a ghostly figure could be seen. Abby grabbed Levi, and they ran to Abby's lake house.

Levi hit one of the rocking chairs on the porch looking back out where the skyline meets the water. He looked over toward the other rocking chair where the doll was already sitting. Her head squeaked and turned to look at Levi. She pointed her little arm out towards the yard and the woods beyond. The ghostly image appeared to float at a snail's pace, getting closer and closer.

He heard the front door open, and he saw it slam shut. He stood up and decided he would go in and check on Abby since he stupidly zoned out. The blood moon shone bright behind him and silhouetted the ghostly figure he didn't see approaching.

"Abby?"

He waited, and his response was met with silence. A loud thump upstairs caused him to jump.

"Abby?" Levi yelled out again.

No response was returned from Abby. He felt a rising sense of dread, as he knew he should go upstairs and face whatever fate awaits him. Fear held him back. Trying to move forward, he knew Abby needed him, but some unseen force continued to prevent him from reaching the stairs. The air became thick and Levi began to shiver as the cold hit him abruptly while his breath could be seen in front of him.

What the fuck, he thought. "I'm coming!" Levi yelled.

As Levi cautiously walked up the stairs, out of the corner of his eye, he saw a mini razor come toward his ankle. Touching himself, he looked at the blood dripping from his hand.

"What the f—"

He dodged the succession of additional attempted cuts and rushed upstairs to get Abby.

"Levi, I know what this looks like, but I didn't do this!"

Abby was sitting on her bed with a steady stream of blood trickling from her right arm with an increased numbing sensation creeping up and shock seeping into her unavoidable consciousness.

"I know. It's that fucking demon doll. Something weird is happening that I can't explain. We need to get out of here. Can you stand? Abby?"

Levi's eyes locked onto Abby, waiting for her to respond. He needed her to say something now more than ever. However, Abby simply slouched, and slumped to the side of her bed, as her eyes drifted to a close.

Shaking Abby gently, he yelled, "Hey, wake up! We have to get out of here! Abby, please." He pleaded with desperation and terror.

Abby stirred slightly, weakened by the loss of blood. Levi observed the crimson stains on her thighs, the white comforter doing its best to soak up the blood spill that continued to flow.

"Abby! Come on, let's go. We can't stay here. We won't make it."

He grabbed her from her armpits to help her stand. Abby mumbled something incoherent as her head lolled. Raising her head and opening her eyes appeared to be a monumental feat. Levi finally gained some footing and helped Abby off of the blood-soaked bed. They moved cautiously toward the top of the stairs and deliberately stepped down slowly to ease the pain of Abby's injuries. Grabbing the car keys from the end table by the door, they stepped outside onto the porch. As they moved toward the car, one of the rocking chairs creaked as it rocked back and forth in quick movements. The doll jumped down. In its little hand sat a small razor with specs of dried blood. Anna moved her arm quickly and the rocking chair and everything in its path cleared like they were being thrown by an invisible malevolent force. The doll moved from in front of the chair in an unnatural and jerky manner. It raised its arm again with the razor blade coming toward them.

"I'm so sorry. I didn't mean to cut you both so deep. Please forgive me." The doll spoke to them as if they have been lifelong friends. "Sometimes I just need to cause a little pain. It's what I was *told* to do. My name is Anna. Oh, wait, I told you that already. I wouldn't step off the porch if I were you. Turn around." Anna motioned for them to look at the yard. There stood a boy that looked unnaturally pale, yet had a slight sparkle. His soulless eyes were staring through Abby and Levi.

"Levi, what is going on?" Abby whimpered.

"I wish I knew," he whispered.

"See? That's why you shouldn't leave just yet. We should watch a movie together! It'll be so fun!" Anna was excited to have friends again. It's been decades since she had any attention.

Anna moved behind them to get them to go inside. "Come on, you two, we don't have all night! I mean, I wish we did, but my brother looks pretty upset and you probably don't have long until..."

"Until what Anna? Just tell us."

"Um, no thank you. Do you have the movie *Scream*? It's so good! Don't you think so, Abby?"

Abby looked at the talking doll with a blank stare. Anna hobbled over and stood in front of her.

"Oh Abby, come on, snap out of it." Anna said as she cut her on her right leg behind her knee.

"Oh gosh, I did it again! Abby, I'm so sorry. My brother told me to." Anna stared up at Abby, expecting her to say something.

Levi went to find *Scream* on one of the streaming services, hoping to distract Anna. He lucked out and found it and promptly started the movie.

"Hey Anna, *Scream* is on for you. Why don't you come in the living room and watch it with us, you know, like you wanted."

Anna ambled her short, stubby doll legs over to the couch in front of the television. She awkwardly hopped up onto the couch and seemed to be mesmerized by the TV. Levi and Abby gave each other knowing looks and backed up near the front door.

Suddenly, knocking could be heard at the front door. It rose in volume and frequency. Levi peeked out of the window and saw nothing. He shrugged and walked back to the living room to sit with Abby, who joined Anna again, without noticing her previous attempt to leave. Anna caused an uncomfortable feeling of dread. They watched *Scream* in silence. Aggressive knocking began again. It was evident that whatever it was, wanted in, but needed an invitation.

Levi got up again and approached the front door, he hesitated with his hand around the doorknob. Shaking, he opened the door with quiet panic. Standing in the doorway was a young male, ghostly figure that nearly sparkled in the moonlight behind him, but this time they saw him. Evil intent oozed from his sinister smile.

The ghost and Anna were quickly upon Levi with Anna's razor providing unwanted, frequent, deep cuts. The ghost held Levi in place with an unknown force. Abby was distraught, as she could do nothing. Tears continued to stream down Abby's face as she tried to wipe them away. Her trembling hand was unable to keep pace with the flood of fear engulfing her.

"Anna, can I go now? You two got what you wanted. You don't need both of us."

"Not quite. I need to get out of this doll, Abby," hissing her response.

"Tony, hold her down." Anna said. The ghostly boy moved swiftly and held Abby in place by standing on her. Abby didn't understand how he could keep her in place since she didn't bear the brunt of his weight. Confusion and fear intertwined. Abby wanted everything to be over. She couldn't fathom surviving this night. Anna was next to Abby, raising her arms and began chanting in an all too familiar voice, which caused Abby to feel sick to her stomach. While lightning outside lit up the shadows in the home, a silhouette in human form stood next to Anna, silently watching them both.

As no one watched Levi, he crept closer to Abby and slammed a crystal vase on the back of the doll's head, knocking her down. He brought the vase down on her head repeatedly, screaming louder each time. Anna's head laid in pieces on the floor next to her headless body. Levi took the razor blade from the doll's hand, shoving it deep inside his pocket. He stood up and looked at Abby. The ghostly boy had disappeared, but a ghostly woman remained.

Abby and Levi scrambled to leave for a second time. The new, ghostly woman cackled as they left. She would follow them outside and follow them forever.

Vindicated Agony

by Kimberly Nicole

Do you ever feel kind of trapped within your own body? Her pain was so severe that day that she couldn't help but daydream about the end of her existence. She didn't want to die...far from it, actually. She wanted to live. But a life like this no longer felt like a life. The physical agony consumed her very being. She dug into her purse, pulled out her prescription bottle, and tossed another pill into her mouth. She washed it down with her lukewarm coffee; the creamer had settled to the top, because she had spaced out for so long, in a blank pain stare, into an abyss of nothingness, that she forgot to drink it. She hated taking them, but it was the only way she could withstand the pain long enough to sit up and do her work. She shook her head, as if attempting to shake off the emptiness that she was stuck within, and looked back down at her computer screen. She began clicking and typing.

She had to get this work done today. Leaving work early yesterday for yet another doctor's appointment put her even further behind than she already was. She desperately needed to keep this job. If she lost this one, she wouldn't be able to afford her rent before being able to find another one. She had already lost three back-to-back. Living in a state that allowed employers to fire without reason was definitely not on her side. If it hadn't been for that fucking accident. That goddamn drunk driver. She sighed. She needed to focus. Back to clicking and typing. An email notification popped up on her screen. She clicked it. Oh fuck, please no. The boss wanted to see her.

Seven Weeks Later

After losing yet another job, she could not afford her bills, and was forced to move back in with her mother. As the excruciating pain continued to take over, she felt herself losing more and more of her mobility. Her depression was at an all-time high. She contemplated the end of it all more often than not now. How could anyone live like this? It hurt to wipe her own ass, to bathe herself, to...breathe. The very thing that kept her alive caused her so much pain that tears would silently slide down her face.

Halloween Eve

"So, is that a yes?! You'll dress up and pass out candy with me!?" her mom cheerfully asked, a goofy ass grin plastered to her adorable face.

"Sure, mom. How could I say no to that face a *third* time?" Penelope replied, with a smart ass expression planted on her own face.

They both laughed.

Halloween Early Evening

"MOM! Where's the candy bowl!?" Penelope belted through their large country home.

"IT'S IN THE KITCHEN!" her mom yelled back from the next room over.

Standing in the middle of the kitchen, Penelope rolls her eyes. "Well, obviously…" she mumbled to the over-cluttered room, and leaned on one of the counters, taking some of her weight off of her black—covered in various stickers—cane. She sucked some of the cool air in through her teeth, then let it all fall back out of her lungs as she grimaced in pain. She was already ready for this night to be over and to be back in her bed, even though it was her most favorite day of the year. Her unending pain truly did suck the joy out of everything.

"Did you find it, Pen?" her mom asked as she made her way back through the kitchen doorway. She can see the beginning signs of more moping on her daughter's face, so she reaches into the correct cabinet for the candy bowl and tells Penelope to go sit down. Her mom wishes she could take her daughter's pain away. But unfortunately, life didn't work like that.

With the candy bowl ready to go by the front door, both ladies dressed in recycled Halloween costumes from several years prior, and a stack of their favorite horror movies on standby, it was time for the festivities to begin.

"Thanks for making me do this, mom. I know I decline more often than not, so it's nice not to be given up on." Penelope says as she gives her mom a gentle, somewhat awkward hug. Penelope never has been much of a hugger. "Which movie should we watch first?" she asked, changing the subject to something less emotionally honest.

"I know what you want me to say, but since it's my choice first, I'm going to go with Insidious!" her mom said, jovial as fuck.

Pen smiled at her mom and nodded, "alright, pop it in." Yes, they still had DVDs.

Just as the movie got past the intro scene, the doorbell chimed throughout their home.

"Trick-or-treaters already?" Penelope said, as though the horror movie marathon was the only reason she was out of bed.

"Let's go!" Her mom exclaimed, jumping up from the couch toward the candy bowl.

Penelope grabbed her cane, grunted her way off the couch, and headed to the front door, where her mom was already standing—candy bowl in hand.

They opened the door to see three children standing there with their candy bags stretched open, ready to receive handfuls of candy. One of them was wearing a Wednesday Addams costume, another was basically identical to Dwight Schrute. *Well, that's adorable as fuck.* And the third was dressed as a vampire.

"Oh my gosh, how adorable!" Penelope's mom exclaimed. "I *love* your costumes!" she added.

Penelope smiled and dropped a handful of various candies into each child's bag. "Stay safe tonight," she mumbled, as she looked toward the end of their driveway and noticed none other than...her old boss. The very person who fired her and caused her life to spiral out of control. Penelope froze. She felt as though her heart may burst out of her chest. It was beating so loud and fast.

She must be the mother of one of these children, Penelope thought. *Must be nice to have such a normal fucking life.* She felt overwhelmed with envy and more enraged than she knew was possible. That's when it hit her—maybe she'd feel better about her own situation, if she could make this bitch miserable, too.

Penelope's mom waved goodbye to the children and to the adults over yonder and then closed the door and put the candy bowl back down on the nearby wooden stool. "Umm...are you okay, Pen? You're acting kind of...ominous. More than usual, I mean," she said, wearing a curious expression on her face.

"Oh, no, I'm fine, mom." Penelope responded, staring into nothingness. "I think I'm going to go for a little walk. Get some fresh air, ya know?" she added.

"Yeah, okay. I'll grab my jacket," her mom responded.

"No, that's okay. I think I'd like to go alone. I won't be gone long." Penelope's rebuttal was weak, but her mother obliged. Penelope grimaced silently as she and her cane made their way out into the dark, chilly evening.

Halloween Night

Penelope kept her distance, but continued to linger behind her ex-boss and the small group of children. She had no clue what she was going to do or if she even intended on doing anything at all. There was this dark cloud drawing her towards this evil woman. This woman who had stolen her livelihood. Robbed her of her last chance to feign normalcy in this lifetime...

She pulled her hood up over her head and curled it around her face, hoping to remain as hidden as possible in the moonlit night.

She noticed her ex-boss pull a set of keys out of her pocket. She wasn't quite sure how long she had been following her. Had it been minutes? Hours? How could she lose track of time so easily? Her pain was screaming gutturally at her, but she kept on going despite it. Then she realized something surprising. The woman was unlocking a door and entering a home with one of the three children. The Dwight.

Holy shit. She must live here. Penelope thought to herself. *I know where she lives...*

November 1st

"All I'm saying is, next time you decide to go out for almost two hours—TAKE YOUR PHONE!" Her mom spoke in a somewhat frantic tone, as though she had been repeating the same thing to unlistening ears for centuries.

"Okay, mom, I will. I really am sorry. I told you, I lost track of time. I didn't mean to be gone that long," Penelope said through a clenched jaw, her agony far more unbearable than its usual level.

Now that Penelope knew where the ex-boss-bitch lived, she couldn't stop herself from daydreaming about all the ways she could potentially take revenge on her. So many bloody, gory options...

Penelope began to doze off, her eyes fluttering, even though she knew she would inevitably lose the fight against another nap. Her constant state of lethargy finally getting the best of her, yet again.

Penelope woke up in a puddle of her own sweat, grimacing in excruciating pain, with vivid memories of a gruesome dream that she had just had. In her dream, she had taken her revenge, and it was oh-so-beautiful.

I know what I'm going to do...

November 2nd

Penelope grabbed her old backpack out of her closet and quietly made her way to the garage in search of their trusty sledgehammer. It would be the perfect tool for her brutal plans. She found it and shoved it into her backpack quickly. She didn't want her mom to catch her doing this. She would have way too many questions, and Penelope was never any good at lying.

With her backpack packed and ready for her *adventure*, now all she had to do was wait for dusk. She knew exactly what time the ex-boss bitch would be getting off work and how long her commute would take. She only hoped that the child took the bus home and didn't rely on boss-bitch for a ride. That would put a serious damper on Penelope's intentions.

She spent the next few hours attempting to play her favorite video game, Dead by Daylight, but found herself struggling to focus, the anticipation of her evening holding the majority of her attention.

Once the sun began setting, she tossed a couple of books and a notebook into her backpack, put her tennis shoes on, tossed her backpack onto her back, and made her way to the front door—hoping to avoid her mother, but having an excuse ready just in case.

Penelope made it outside unnoticed and started toward her destination, feeling far more excited than nervous, almost as if she were headed to some sort of celebration rather than the brutal attack she had been daydreaming—and dreaming—about.

As she approached her destination, she decided she should check the backdoor. Penelope crossed her fingers that it would be unlocked. She reached for the door and grabbed the handle. It twisted. The door opened. She went inside and shut the door, quiet as a mouse. She was 99% sure there was no one else here, but wanted to be quiet just to be on the safe side.

She found a bench near the front door and sat down, her pain levels battling for her attention, despite the adrenaline that she was experiencing. She pulled a book and the sledgehammer out of her backpack and sat it down beside her. With the sledgehammer in her lap, ready to go, she opened up her book and attempted to read. It usually warded off her pain ever so slightly and she hoped it would do so now, as well.

Roughly twenty minutes later, she finally heard a car pull up into the driveway. It was almost her time to *shine.* She placed her bookmark into her book and sat it down beside her. Then she pulled her Ghostface hood over her head and wrapped the Ghostface part around her face, picked up the sledgehammer, and waited. She opted to leave her cane out back, because she was attempting to remain anonymous, and she knew that her ex-boss would know it was her if she saw her cane.

She heard a key enter the lock and turn. *Click.* The doorknob began turning and the door creaked open.

Shit! The boy was with her. *Fuck!*

What was she going to do? She had to think fast.

"You, sit over there. Now," Penelope said to the boy, while aiming the sledgehammer at his head.

"Please, no. Take whatever you want. We don't care. Just leave us alone," said the ex-boss bitch.

"All I want is for you to feel the same agony that I feel. The same level of fear, disappointment, pain, and hopelessness," Penelope responded as the boy sat down.

"What? Who *are* you?"

"Your worst fucking nightmare, bitch," Penelope said as she began smashing the sledgehammer into her spine repeatedly. The pitch of the woman's screams was an audible expression of how Penelope had felt every day for the last seven years. She didn't want to kill her. But she wanted her to hurt like she did. To be debilitated like she was. To get fired like she had been fired...

The boy cried and screamed, "please stop!" over and over, through a snot and tear covered face.

"Now you get to hurt, too," Penelope said to the woman as she loaded up her backpack and walked out the back door.

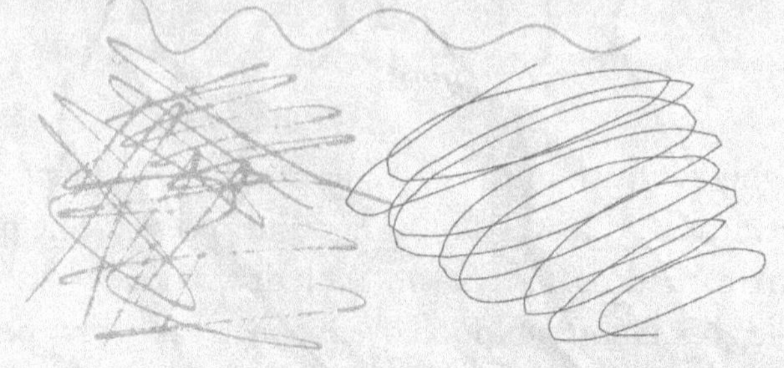

THE FAMILY O'FAOLAIN

BY AJ HUMPHREYS

"*Is mac tíre é fear*"

Those are the old Gaelic words carved into his headstone. The irony of their meaning not lost on me.

I had expected the masonry to be more opulent. Instead, it's a simple black granite rectangle. Though, the Gaelic script is inlaid with a shimmering silver paint that brings the stone to life beneath the moon's luminescence. Evoking a treasure-like glint across the polished lettering in the wee hours of this *Sauin* morning.

The cemetery is secluded on a tiny bluff, hidden amongst the last pines of the Rocky Mountains, before the air gets too thin for them to grow.

Our little family plot rests as quietly as any other grave site. However, the ambiance of the mountain air is rather different. It's a louder silence, almost palpable. At 11,000 feet above sea level, there isn't much around adding to the senses, so the absence of sensory details becomes more pronounced.

As a child, Halloween had evoked mixed feelings in me. It had been my favorite holiday, but because it signaled the coming of Sauin the following morning, the night was often filled with words from my father that instilled trepidation and fear.

Then Mom died.

A rockslide struck her car, sending her careening over the edge of the mountain pass. We'd later learn the incident was caused by the unsanctioned blasting and construction of some rich asshole's holiday cabin.

She had been on her way home with candy for us. It was Halloween, and I was nine.

Instead, that night, there was no candy. No one to look out for us. No one to sneak us out for trick-or-treating in the next real town over. And certainly, no one to make sure the carvings of the old world were replicated exactly as they should have been.

Which is how we lost our youngest brother, Cillian.

So, it felt like Halloween died that day too.

All that remained was Sauin.

Which was not so much a holiday, but a marker designating a looming obligation.

Yet, Dad never acted like the day had become tainted for him, as if he actually had the human emotional capacity to miss my mother or brother.

Not that he ever remarried or sought to replace Cillian. After all, he didn't have to. He'd done his duty and sired the necessary number of sons for the inevitable ritual. Three. Maybe that explained why loss or grief never debilitated the man.

Without intervention, it would have been several more decades before our father departed this world.

But there had been an intervention. And now those of us remaining will take part in a ritual at day's end that should have loomed far in the future. A blood right owed to our ancestry.

Or so we'd been led to believe.

Despite the loss of our youngest brother, my two remaining siblings saw this event as a competition with a prize to be won.

Both were surprised to learn of our father's passing, yet each acted almost giddy. As if the chance to have *his* responsibilities were not the set of shackles forged through the curse of lies that I know them to be.

And there's no convincing my brothers otherwise. They have too much of dear old dad in them.

My older brother Colin, who got too much freedom after Mom died, never saw the wickedness in our father.

My younger brother Conor received too little. Treated like a rare and delicate artifact. Or the last great hope of a dying nation.

Then there's me, Ciaran, left somewhere floating in that forgettable space between. Yet, that never stopped Dad from using me as his personal punching bag when he could remember I existed.

But those days are gone and this early morning rendezvous will mark the first time that all three O'Faolain boys will have been in the same place in over seven years.

"Ciaran!" Conor's obtuse shout fractures the crisp mountain silence. I can't quite see him, but his silhouette lumbers down the hillside trail to where I sit with Dad's headstone.

Dad made Conor into everything Colin and I weren't—his ideal heir.

Yet, the big galoot lacked any sense of decorum for a graveyard at two am on a Monday.

"Oofff. Hey there, little brother." The words expel from my mouth as he lifts me off the ground in a bear hug.

The guy has the body of an All-Pro middle linebacker with the brain of a Chess Grand Champion; and what did he do with all that?

He was a stockbroker.

He had a penthouse apartment in the city and a lavish lifestyle that featured drugs, sex workers, and several illicit business practices. The sort that added an extra zero to the end of his bank account balance, but sacrificed so much more. Like his heavy-handed influence on investing in companies that destroyed the environment in favor of profit margins.

A regular wolf of Wall Street.

One who's strong enough to squeeze the life out of me here and now if he wanted to try. But, even if he did, try that is, that doesn't mean I'd just let him succeed.

Once he finally finishes sizing me up, Conor plops me down to find the slender man presence of my older brother, 'The Politician'—more importantly, *The House Majority WHIP*.

"Evening, Congressman O'Faolain. Soft-footed as ever."

There was no escaping Colin. If he wanted to get through a door, he'd tread lightly and quietly, slipping through and pouncing the instant he saw his opening.

His handshake is calculated and strategic. He's feeling me out. Trying to get a read on my headspace this evening. He'll play nice. He'll be my big brother. He'll don the sheep's clothing. As he always does.

Like most politicians, Colin sought power and influence. Both things he has accumulated in spades, despite what, or who, he's discarded along the way.

Though, I'm already prepared for the wolf who thinks that his tattered, sheepish veil is enough to catch me unsuspecting.

"Ciaran. Good to see you. When will our guide be arriving?"

Then there's me. The rebel, the runt, the 'yellow dog' as the old man's inner circle took to calling me.

While my brothers did exactly as my father had blueprinted for them—move away, learn, grow, and become the so-called 'big shots' from the Podunk, tiny mountain town of Alma, Colorado—I stayed.

I have a nice little operation going. I run a bar-slash-*hodgepodge store,* as I call it.

Have a beer? Great!

Maybe a burger and some fries? Sure thing!

Need toilet paper, bottled water, you name it; just go to the back half of the building. There, I've got just about anything one could imagine lining the racks and shelves. Camping gear, hiking supplies, groceries, and, of course, tourist trap souvenirs.

In the eyes of my family, this made me invisible.

I enjoyed that invisibility. It consumed my identity. A man too plain to ingrain into someone's memory.

With my inconspicuous lifestyle, I bore witness to the world without our father's lies tinting my perspective.

Sure, I saw what our old man wanted us to see. But I observed far beyond that.

I saw what *The Otherside* had done to us. Our family. Not to mention the world.

I saw the truth. I saw humanity. I saw monsters.

Soon, I learned more about the spirits and *so-called ills* that Dad so desperately worked to prevent from accessing our world. Unfortunately, he was too fixated on what he wanted to see that he never witnessed the monsters already amongst us.

Like the one whose selfish interests stole my mother from me.

An event that had a ripple effect on Cillian and cost him his life before he'd ever finished shedding his baby teeth.

They came that Sauin morning, as they always do. But without my mother's hands there to aid the smallest of us, Cillian's poorly etched lantern failed to survive the night.

And we never saw him again.

The world beyond these mountains is a soft place. I know this because I can see how it has whittled away the stone-like strength my brothers once possessed. Their comfortable lives have sheltered them from the dangers lying in wait.

Hazards our family created over generations.

For we have never been guardians. No, our ancestors raised slavers and executioners.

These are natural truths on par with gravity. I know the *real* facts concerning *The Otherside*. I have learned what the true balance must look like across *The Fracture*.

Something my father couldn't see. Or perhaps refused.

Irrespective of this, Colin had a question, and I knew to answer it, "Soon. It's still quarter-to-three, and you know as well as I, she won't arrive a second sooner."

"Somebody's been brushing up on all the rules! I'm surprised, big bro!" Conor tries again to throw me off balance with his big meat paw, thwacking me across the back. I let him think he's knocked me off balance, that he's getting to me. That's right where I want him. Unsuspecting of his diminutive older brother.

"Never needed to. Dad made sure I knew them, same as you."

Our father was just more violent with me.

The man had to test his limits. Know what was too far, and not repeat such things with his prized child.

While some scars manifest only in the mind, they are all too present in our wisdom.

The quiet autumn night remains still. At this elevation, the moon's glow is brighter, the stars are infinite, and the darkness is quieter, yet filled with far more color than ordinary shadows could ever imagine.

Our breaths quietly meld into the air, shimmering like spirits escaping our bodies. Time passes and those tiny specters are all that break the peace between the three of us.

A place once teeming with life rests as quiet as the graves upon which we sit.

Good Sauin, Brothers O'Faolain.

"Woah. So that's what it's like. Never expected it to be so intrusive," Conor says, searching inside his head as if he'd be able to pinpoint the voice that only spoke inside our skulls.

I had almost forgotten that neither of my brothers has spoken with Cailleach before. I find her speech intrusive as well, but something I've been able to grow accustomed to.

The wolf pads out silently behind us. She hasn't changed since the last time I laid eyes on her.

Cailleach's fur is ghastly pale, bordering on an icy blue beneath the moonlight. One eye is slit shut, the mark of a battle from stories both ancient and harrowing that I couldn't care less about reciting. Her other eye stares blankly through each of us with a milky hue. Her teeth look stained. Red, like wine, but I know, and so too should my brothers, that those are not the stains of fermented grapes.

As the fracture weakens, I return to ye. Upon this year, we mark the selection of the next 'seachd.' So, have the O'Faolain guarded the doorway between the realms of beasts and those of The Other for many centuries, so soon shall one of ye three be responsible for serving as a vessel until such a time that the mortal coil should reach its end.

The wolf's voice echoes like that of an old crone throughout our minds. It's raspy and shrill and still retains that thick and speedy Northern Irish accent. The Cailleach, or Cylee as we'd grown to call her as boys, has been a part of our family since our Great-Great-Great-Grandfather came over from Ireland all those years ago.

Have you all brought your carvings?

Both my brothers heft large hiking packs filled with a bulbous gourd and the necessary provisions.

I have a smaller pack.

"You do know how long your fire has to burn, right?"

I scoff at Colin's veiled criticism. Just enough to make him think I'm foolish, rather than needlessly arouse his suspicions.

He rolls his eyes, as expected, and hefts the pack atop his fancy outerwear-laden body. Conor just laughs.

Then ye must begin.

So, each of us removes an oversized turnip from our packs. All three gourds etched with our family's sigil upon their edifices.

The wolf's head.

Colin is the first to light his lantern. He's using a LARGE candle with a thick wick that should last the day.

Conor's approach employs a citronella tankard. Hard to say if it'll be enough, but surely it will be heavy. And that will wear on my brother, despite his bulging muscles.

Cylee saunters off ahead of us, disappears onto the winding dirt road that leads to our destination. My brothers quickly follow, forgetting about me and my half-sized gourd, which burns with an unnatural glow, brighter than either of the other men's.

Our destination is the DeCaLiBron Loop. Four successive mountains interconnected, all peaking out above 14,000 feet of elevation.

Along our two-and-a-half hour journey to the base of the trail, shadows shift and slide just beyond the trinity of glowing lanterns, as if veiled dancers rehearsing before curtain call.

A small voice inside me almost wishes that one of my brothers, if not both, would just allow their torches to burn out. But that would be taking the easy way out, which would dissolve the contract.

I'd come too far to renege on my share of the covenant I'd entered.

Vigilance is paramount along our trek through darkness. The threats lurking in the fading ebony landscape will remain until the sun reaches apogee. Though, our lanterns must remain lit despite the raw pink glow announcing the sun's arrival on the horizon.

And they do.

The sun finally sheds the mountainous skyline, embracing us with a warm fall glow as we reach the trailhead.

There's no cloud cover, and the direct sunlight feels good. But the air is so thin that a biting cold gnaws at us with each blustering gust.

Without the intense breath of shadows, I can see my brothers more clearly. It's obvious they haven't been up a mountain in some time, as they lag further behind me.

I think about calling them out. Razzing them a hare with a brotherly jab, but I resist the urge. Plus, I'd have to slow down for them to even hear me.

And that doesn't serve the plan.

Halfway up, the dirt path switches to loose stone. The trail is easy to discern, but many of the rocks are capable of shifting underfoot. I hear one of my brothers lose their footing and tumble. I don't care to check. The trail *is* safe, for the most part, but that doesn't mean one wrong step on a precarious rock couldn't lead to a twisted ankle or a torn ACL.

A stone gingerly shifts beneath my weight as I take the curve of a violent switchback. This is the exact spot I've been waiting for. Having hiked this trail more times than I can count, I know it like the back of my hand. Here, I am secluded and hidden.

I kneel down as if going to tie my shoe. Instead, adjusting the offending stone to sit more precariously before continuing up the mountain.

Minutes pass before I hear the sound I've been anticipating. "Ciaran! Help!"

I look down and see just how far I've traveled since sabotaging the trail. Feigning shock, I march back down to them. But I take longer than my brothers would like to reach their anxious expressions.

"Conor slipped on this stone and twisted his ankle."

"Actually, I think it's my knee. It's pretty fucked." My younger brother adds as he sits clutching his injured leg.

"Are you going to quit, then? You probably should. Don't you think?" I say, knowing how much that will motivate Conor to press onward.

"Oh, I'm not giving up that easy." The brute shoots back.

He pulls a long stick from his pack, meant for kindling, and utilizes it as a splint for his ankle. He limps slowly, but impressively, and expectedly.

He won't stop.

The hike from here will appear uneventful, but it's where I begin my psychological warfare against Colin.

I let him heft Conor up the steeper parts of the trail while I jog up and down *'looking for any more precarious situations'*—of which there will be none. But, I can see the doubt creeping into my brother's eyes as he realizes I'm not out of breath at this altitude despite all my physical exertion and weak stature.

He, on the other hand, has been breathing heavily for some time, and when I tell him, "Only a mile to go,"—considering we've been traversing the mountain for at least three miles already—I can see that neither brother is thrilled with this n ews.

Along the last quarter mile, I pull ahead, knowing that a private interlude at the summit will do me wonders.

Colin is the first to reach me.

I've been at the summit of Mount Democrat—the first of the four peaks of the DeCaLiBron Loop—for nearly thirty minutes. It's another forty before Conor limps his way to the top.

The sun's position tells me it's just after mid-day.

There, atop the mountain, we each take delight in our lanterns surviving the ordeal.

They *will* survive until nightfall.

And once the setting sun finally turns the sky over to the darker shades of the heavens above, Cylee's voice penetrates our thoughts once more

The time is nigh, brothers three.

All three fires remain lit.

🍄 🍄 🍄

"What are *you* doing here?" My father had said to me with such disdain.

"Putting all your lessons to use." I chided him matter-of-factly.

The scowl across his face was his own, not the spirit to which he lent his body. But *there* was the wolf. Still sat at my father's side, staring with its lone eye.

I strode over to my father, who sat amongst piles and piles of texts, studying *The Otherside*, preparing for the cold winter to come when *The Fracture* between worlds would widen.

He looked down at the wolf. Perplexed, and heaved himself upward with an *umpf* that catches him by surprise.

"Not feeling like yourself, old man?"

That's the thing. He does look older, and he must be feeling it, as fear washes across his face.

"You know, Cylee's agreement was meant to bring balance and peace to *both* worlds. But I've seen what man has done to this world that had once belonged to her and her kind."

My father slumps back into his seat, his breath labored. He had not aged a day throughout the entirety of my life, but now the years were peeling off of him. His skin sagged, his eyes grew dull, and his hair fell away in wispy strands.

"What have you done?"

"What needed to be done, Father. I have already forged a pact with Cylee, but you see, her kind are sticklers for ritual formality. I cannot have *all* her power until you've died, and I've won the trials, but we were able to *expedite* the process."

"You c-c-can't." He stammers out.

"Oh, but I have. You thought Conor or Colin would hold the balance? No. They'll just continue to destroy our world the way they have, with their mortal responsibilities. I, on the other hand, will help Cylee and her kind restore our world. No more climate change. No more toxic waste. No more overpopulation. No more *needless* death."

"Th-th-th —"

"Save your breath, Father, you don't have many left. In fact, I better do the deed before you succumb to *natural* causes. I do have an obligation to fulfill, after all."

An apex predator survives best because it leaves nothing alive to threaten it.

With my father gone, only two men threatened my vision for the future.

Upon darkness's reclamation of the land, an untimely Hunter's Moon fills the sky. Its deep orange glow mimics the flickering flames within our gourds.

The Fracture opens in mid air above us. A tear in the fabric of reality connecting this plane of existence with that of *The Otherside.*

Strength fills my veins.

I stomp on Conor's lantern first. Smashing it to pieces and collapsing the citronella canister within.

My bones break. Fuse back together and lengthen. An itch coats my skin as thick white hairs erupt from my pores.

Colin is too stunned to stop me from punting his oversized gourd into the night looming over the mountainside.

My face is the last to change. Searing waves of electricity remold my jaws, lips, and nose.

Conor's in too much pain to move, and Colin bears a stupid expression that boils my blood. He had underestimated me. Like always.

Before my receding fingers have melded into claws, I snap my fingers. The last lantern, my lantern, erupts in flame.

A surge of unfathomable cold erupts from the widening blue waves of *The Fracture*. Pulses of something eldritch and violent spill into the air and the lycanthropy takes hold.

Colin is the first to go. That stupid look twisting his features needed to be wiped off the face of the Earth.

I see a pathetic little boy where Conor sat. Sniveling and crying. Unfit to bear the O'Faolain family duties.

I drink from their viscera after it's all said and done. It tastes like godly nectar flowing between the elongated snout where my nose and mouth had once been as a mortal man.

Then comes the final transaction.

Cylee gives me her bite and the entire world falls away. She drinks from my blood, and then I hers once more. Just as I had before disposing of dear old dad.

When my eyes open, and I lick my lips, I take in the carnage through the eyes of a man rather than those of a beast.

I am the one who will restore the balance between this world and that of the spirits from *The Otherside*. Those who man displaced out of fear and ignorance so many centuries ago.

The family motto scribed on our father's grave returns to mind. And though I know its meaning to be, *man is wolf to man,* I can't help but chuckle at the irony as I whisper them aloud, sealing my pact.

"Is mac tíre é fear."

Highway Call

by Jospeh Murnane

I was seventeen when I joined the volunteer fire department. It was against the rules, but I made a strong case, and we lived in a small, quiet town. I won't say which town—just that it's on the east coast, near I-95.

I was already on my own, hundreds of miles from any relatives, the only exception being my newborn son. I won't reveal his name, but we'll just call him Jay.

Anyway, I was a kid in a new place with a kid of my own and everything to prove. Not just to show everybody around that I could handle this, but to prove I was worthy of this precious, fragile little ball of human that happened to have the shit luck of being born to me as his dad. I didn't just want to be *capable*. I wanted to be somebody, so that if he or anybody else saw me walking down the street, they'd know I was there to help.

I wanted to be a hero.

I wanted to be *his* hero.

I had a couple of friends already riding Engine 40, so they brought me up to the brass and they called the whole company together. I talked to the lieutenants and the captain for a bit, then they gave me a tour of the firehouse. I felt like a little kid when they let me climb up into the front seat of that massive yellow engine. I'd never seen a yellow rig before. Our town had a green one, too.

After that, I waited on the other side of these heavy oak double doors while fifty-five strangers sat in chairs on the other side, taking a vote. If they had decided not to take me, it wouldn't have been about me, just that I was too young. Still, it felt like they were weighing me as an entire person. If they hadn't accepted me, it would have felt like passing judgment on my worth, on my very *capacity* to be of service to another person. On my potential to be a *hero*. If they said no, it was going to crack me right apart.

I was smart, but damn, was I stupid.

Cut to a half hour later, and they called me into the room, stood me up in front of everybody, and swore me in. I'd never taken an oath before. It made me feel like a knight, and tears actually spilled out when they gave me a badge, numbered 1 271.

That number was mine now. It would tell the world that I was actually part of it. I'd never felt like part of anything before.

Everybody in the room stood and clapped for me, bunched around and shook my hand, introduced themselves. I lost their names as soon as I heard them—I was just too wrapped up in my own pounding pulse, my swelling heart. I'd come to know them all, but that would happen later.

Outside of time spent at home or at the kitchen job that actually paid me, that firehouse became my whole world. I hung out there after work, trained on my off days, ate there, brought little Jay down for big weekly dinners that we all prepared together. I got CPR certified first, then I started working on other certifications. I learned how to pack hose and do it fast. I hiked up and down the stairs of an eight story training building in sixty-five pounds of turnout gear, learning how to push through while still keeping my lungs in check. The last thing you want in a real situation is to suck down all your air before you even get where you need to go.

The better your conservation, the more trips you could make up and down the stairs before your tank went dry. So despite my screaming muscles, all I ever did was pray for one more trip. In the shit, that one more trip could make all the difference, and I didn't want to be a volunteer forever.

I wanted to go to the real show, live in that heat for as long as I could, make Jay as proud of me as I knew I'd always be of him.

So I never stopped pushing, not even when I slipped on the sixth floor one day, cracked my helmet on the thirty-inch halligan I was carrying, biting my tongue so hard I thought I bit the tip right off. I just let the blood roll down my chin, did three more trips up and down before my tank told me I was allowed to quit.

I wish I'd just gone home that day, found some other way to be of use to my community, but like I said, I was part of something now. At the time, nothing could have made me give that pager up.

We all had them on our belts. Volunteers don't have scheduled shifts. They have pagers. No matter where we went, we were always on call, ready to drop whatever we were doing at any moment. When you're a kid stuck on a grill, the feeling of looking your manager in the eye, telling them "I've got to go," in the middle of the dinner rush and following that screaming black box on your hip out onto the street? There's nothing like it. For me and my friends, it was a rebuke of our menial drudgery. What were they going to tell us? No? Don't go fight the fire? Even if they did, we'd be out the door anyway, piling into Jerry's car or sprinting down the road on foot if he didn't have any gas in the tank. We wanted to be heroes, and no balding kitchen manager with a coke habit was going to get between us and a shot at some real action.

But we weren't at work when the highway call came in. We were at Eric's house.

Eric hated his day job just like the rest of us, but working at a wine shop had its perks—namely, all the inventory that mysteriously found its way from the warehouse to Eric's refrigerator. This time, he had a few dozen small bottles of this horrendous dessert wine. It was cloying, syrupy stuff that was harder to force down than cough medicine, but we did our best with it, anyway. If there was any saving grace that evening, it had to be that we couldn't drink it fast enough to get wasted, so we were mostly sober when all our pagers started howling at each other, sending us off into the night.

Six of us piled into Eric's red Camry as he started the car and kicked on the flashing red lights he'd mounted to the windshield. There was nothing official about them, just some lights he'd ordered from the internet, but the illumination still served to herd slower traffic out of our way as we raced to the firehouse. Jerry was spread across our laps in the back seat, and the sickening too-sweet odor of his wine breath threatened to make me gag. If I think about it, I can still smell it.

We skidded to a halt on the street, spilling out of the car as fast as we could without tangling ourselves up, and sprinted through the open bay door. Along the south wall sat a row of open lockers holding turnout gear and equipment. At the very end of the row, my heart caught in my throat at the sight of my own name having been added to the wall above my newly assigned locker. Jerry winked at me.

"Surprise!" he said. "They set that up for you last night."

I nodded dumbly, stuck in place for a moment before the adrenaline rose in my chest, and I went about pulling all the new gear on as fast as I could. I promised myself I'd live up to that locker, my name on the wall, my own bunker jacket. Little did I know it was just a fucking costume, at least as far as I deserved it.

I took my place in the back of the truck, and the driver engaged the siren as we pulled out of the garage. It wasn't far, maybe four miles to the highway ramp we set up on. A lilac minivan was crushed to half its size off the shoulder. Apparently, this van had gotten onto the highway heading the wrong direction a full seventeen miles away. To this day, I don't know how they even made it that far, let alone why they chose that course to begin with.

We beat the ambulances there, so the older heads went straight for the wreckage to see what they could do about extricating the occupants, while I and a few others went about securing the lanes, placing cones, shepherding traffic around us to avoid another collision.

With my cones set up, I made my way toward the crushed van, past the semi-truck driver that had hit them, a rugged looking old man crying out in apology. I was about ten yards from the van when I saw her.

A woman stood in the grass out in front of the vehicle, awash in dying headlights. Her back was to me, but I could see her pointing out into the trees. It was as though she felt me looking, and she turned to face me. I almost threw up right then.

The bottom half of her jaw was ripped away. Her clothes were torn and smoking, and blood flowed in curtains down her legs, seemingly kept upright by the pure desperation in her eyes.

I tried to call out to Jerry. Why wasn't anybody helping her? Either he didn't hear me, or he was just too wrapped up in the other vital duties he had to perform.

So it had to be me. She was looking at *me* for help, still pointing into the trees. Her tongue bobbed and flicked uselessly against her throat as she tried to speak. Panic seized me and I found myself rooted in place, incapable of any action. I needed to run to her, get her off her feet, do something—*anything* if I was going to stabilize her.

But my training hadn't come that far yet, and I was a terrified, arrogant kid. I just fucking stood there. I couldn't hear anything anymore, the sirens and shouts muted beneath the weight of my own fear. Everything around me seemed to be happening in fast forward, save for the woman and those ugly dark pools spreading across her yellow sundress.

"What the fuck are you doing, man?" Jerry was suddenly at my side. I turned to point at the woman, to beg him to do something because I couldn't, but she was gone. There was nobody standing there, pointing off into the trees.

I didn't see the ambulances arrive either, but now there were three of them. A pair of paramedics were pulling a woman from the passenger side of the crumpled van. A woman in a yellow sundress. Clearly, unequivocally dead.

I didn't answer Jerry. Instead, I turned and ran. I sprinted all the way home and locked the door, collapsed to the floor with my back against it. Maybe an hour after that, my phone started ringing. The voicemails were surprisingly supportive. I wasn't the first person to break and flee their first taste of real carnage. But that wasn't what I was running from.

It wasn't until the next day, when the driver woke up screaming about his son, that anybody went back to the scene and ventured into the woods. They found the dead boy just inside the treeline, the drag marks behind him indicating that he'd tried to crawl back toward the flashing lights on the road. He was four years old, and he almost made it.

I never called anybody else in the department back. I returned my gear when nobody else was there, left my badge on the bar. I quit the kitchen job too, and we ended up packing up and leaving town for somewhere without so much blood dripping from its guardrails.

But she followed me here. The bloody woman with her flapping tongue and pointing, accusatory finger was always with me. Only now she wasn't pointing at the trees. Her desperate eyes were fixed on my son like she wanted to take him from me. And the worst part? I think he saw her, too.

I could have helped her boy before it was too late, and I'd forever accept her judgment if she would just leave mine alone. I could have made the difference I'd always hoped I would. I could have saved a life.

But I didn't, because I'm a fucking coward.

I needed to be stronger than that for him, though. A father sacrifices for their children. That's why I let her in.

A few months after we moved, I knew what I had to do. I gave my sleeping wife one last kiss on the cheek and crept into Jay's room. The ghost was standing over his crib, gurgling wistfully. I joined her, and together we watched him breathe, scrunching his little face through a dream.

"I know you don't want to hurt him," I whispered. "Take me instead."

Her attention snapped up, cloudy eyes locking onto mine, her head cocked to the side inquisitively.

"You heard me," I said. "I failed. I never should have been on that highway, but it isn't his fault, is it? Doesn't he deserve a life? So just do it. Take me and leave my boy alone."

And that was all it took. I felt a gust of cold wind, and I was alone in my son's room.

But not in my body.

For ten years now, I've been a passenger in my own vessel. I can feel my hands, but I cannot move them. I can see through the windows of my eyes, but it's not up to me when they open. As the years pass, I can feel more and more of myself fading away.

But sometimes, she whispers to me, pulls me up from the growing darkness, runs my hand through my son's messy hair, and I am grateful. At least this way, I still get to watch him grow. Maybe not the way I would have hoped, but I know that he's safe now, and from my distant vantage point, I still get to be a part of that.

And it might just be for the best. He's a smart, happy boy, and he really seems to love the new me.

Maybe I'm a better mother than I ever would have been a father.

But I'm still here, son.

Do you see me?

Up North

by Svea Nietzke

Her cell phone was on the table with the notification that Lara Horne's genetic results from Family Tree.com were ready. Her parents, James, and Olivia Anderson, never told her anything about her birth family. They always said it didn't matter because she was safe and loved. She was their daughter. Blood didn't mean anything. Lara sat crying on a dining chair, deciding whether to open it now or wait until her husband, Robert, and ten-year-old daughter, Emma, got home from the grocery store. Her beautiful, blond-haired daughter just had her birthday. Lara's hands trembled as she wiped away her tears with tissues. She got up and clenched her teeth; she just had to see what it said. Because of her hands, she almost dropped the phone. Maybe it wasn't time yet. Lara collected herself just enough to punch in her password and get into the app. She closed her eyes and flipped her phone down. The sickly sweet smell of her cherry macarons and home-brewed autumn spiced latte filled the kitchen. The scent would usually have been lovely, but it clung to her sweat-soaked, white designer blouse. Lara inhaled the cloying odors to calm herself down.

There were many times she fantasized about what her birth parents and family were like. Focusing on details that didn't matter. Did they go grocery shopping in a store in summer or farmer's markets? Did they go to football games regularly or visit museums? Did they live in a mansion or a modest townhouse? Did they live somewhere that could grill an egg on the sidewalk or somewhere with brutal winters? The list could go on. Her adoptive parents were average, just going through life with a routine. They never even took her on vacation. Despite their boring lifestyle, they always gave her love and supported her. Some parents would discourage their daughters from becoming fashion designers with dreams of owning upscale, modern boutiques. Not James and Olivia. They showed interest and checked on her when she was creating her clothes as a teen. Before getting her driver's license, she begged them to see shops around the Milwaukee area to research classic and trending styles. They didn't feel like they were being dragged along. The only thing that mattered was her happiness. They had enough money to pay for her art education. No matter how tired they were after coming home from work, they comforted her so she could stop obsessing over her design projects that had tight deadlines, making sure she went to bed with a peaceful mind. Lara knew they were proud of her no matter what, but their faces glowed when she went to her first store opening. Her parents even went outside their comfort zones to attend fashion shows across the US that featured their daughter's lines when she established herself in the world of extravagant fabrics.

Guilt filled her with the need for knowledge. Why wouldn't they tell her about anything? Were they afraid that she would replace them with people who gave her up when she was a little baby? She could never do that. They must have had good reason to make that sacrifice. She thought perhaps her mom and dad thought she would reject them for her birth family. She could never do that. Lara needed to stay positive, but her anxiety was starting to take over. While breathing deep breaths, she rotated her head from side to side and around. It took too much effort to stretch her arms. This was good enough. Doing these techniques was strenuous. She needed this. Sadie, their German Shepherd, trotted from the front room and then nudged Lara's elbow with her long, soft snout. Sadie was empathetic and also trained in protection work. If anything happened, Sadie would be there to help, either emotionally or physically. Lara opened her eyes and pushed Sadie away gently.

"Not right now, girl." Sadie lay down underneath the table as Lara worked herself up again. She'd always have a hole inside her without knowing the truth. Screaming in emotional agony, she clenched her eyes shut again, grabbed her phone, flipping it back up. She tried counting to three before opening them again. That was useless because she did it suddenly, and the results kept her wide-eyed.

Lara smiled. Her lips were still a little salty from the fallen tears. Page one broke down her genetic makeup—100% German, specifically from the Black Forest region. The map showed they were there for one thousand years before her ancestors immigrated to the US in 1845. It showed they arrived in New York before settling across the country into Wisconsin. The app didn't show cities; that would only be under the contact information section.

She was a little more at peace. This meant her children were part German too, besides Polish and Czech on her husband's side. Her husband will be happy for her. He knew how much this meant to her. They had been married for twenty years. Lara met Robert when they were eighteen at a party on a Friday night. They weren't huge drinkers; they were more into floating around the host's house to talk and joke around. She wouldn't stay long because she had a dress to prepare for a class, but he spontaneously asked her to dance to a hip-hop song with him. Not long after that, they began dating. Dating led to being engaged three months later.

To celebrate, they had gone up to his dad's cottage in Ziigwan, which was up north. If a town doesn't have a major sports team, college, or a swanky suburb, Wisconsin calls it "Up North." His dad had no idea they were going, which was risky. It was January, and Robert's dad wasn't into doing outdoor winter activities. They drove down long, straight highways, ending up on a stretch of snow-covered gravel roads until they arrived at the cottage. The snow was deep, going past their shins. They struggled to walk through, but they held each other's hands while they held shovels in the other. It was thirty-five degrees, and no wind. Lara loved that it was cold but wasn't bitter. It seemed the trees and houses were dressed in white silk. Once they shoveled a path to the front door, they got their luggage and admired the wilderness underneath the shining full moon. They embraced each other, gazing into each other's faces, knowing their love would last forever. It was one of the most romantic nights of their lives, but also the most frightening.

When they were inside unpacking their clothes, a truck drove up the long, wide driveway. Lara had never feared anything and didn't have a reason to. On the other hand, Robert became nervous when he heard it and saw it through the window. He put his coat and everything back on to see what they wanted.

"Please stay here," he told her. Lara didn't listen and got her winter gear back on. Robert grasped her arm as they went to see what the people wanted.

With a puzzled look, he noticed there wasn't anyone in the truck, but found a trail of footprints leading into the woods, along with drag marks. Lara's eyes traced the dried blood up and down the trail. It looks like we have poachers, at least I hope, she thought.

They felt compelled to follow, hiding behind a tangle of bare bush branches. They had to know what the people were up to if they were on his dad's land without permission. There was a clearing where the trees were bowing down around an altar. Slowly, Lara and Robert began to sense more was happening here. A man was slumped upside down on the flat stone fixture. Bells rang from a short distance and grew louder, becoming ear-shattering as men dressed in fur approached closer. The sound of the bells was both hypnotic and unbearable. When it stopped, Robert and Lara remembered where they were and what they suspected was happening. Lara opened her mouth to scream but realized that she would get them killed; her throat felt stuck, trying to swallow her fear.

Robert whispered, "Lara? We can't die out here." He reached over to Lara, tugging on her arm. They didn't move, though they wanted to. That man on the altar was either dead or knocked out. The cult chanted, "Abnoba, Abnoba, Abnoba." Their voices crawled all over their souls. The time went from being non-existent to rushing like a flash flood. The man struggled to get back up and suddenly bolted through the deep snow. He was caught by an invisible force, floating then struggling like a fly stuck in a spider's web into the night air.

"Robert!" She whispered harshly, "We need to go now! Something is going to kill him!" Robert looked over, scoping out the dangers that prevented them from escaping.

"If we walk inside our footsteps carefully, we shouldn't make noise. Keep low, okay?" Lara nodded at him. She looked behind her and saw a beautiful woman riding a giant wild boar. She raised her hands; in thousands of places, he was being sliced. He was unrecognizable; blood poured into the white snow, and then he fell into lumps. At that point, Robert and Lara ran, shaking for a few feet until the members caught t hem.

It was time they fought, and they did, writhing the entire way until they were brought before the woman. They couldn't scream, they couldn't speak. It was even hard for the both of them to breathe. Men pulled out prehistoric-looking knives, probably made out of human bone. Lara squeezed Robert's hand, believing this was the last time they would be together alive. Before the men stuck the knives into their throats, the woman bellowed.

"I am Abnoba. Do you know who I am?" Lara and Robert shook their heads no, not looking into her predator-like, bright green eyes. They could feel the wild boar's breath on them.

"I am the Goddess who came here with those who worshipped me in the Black Forest. I protect it with might and demand the sacrifice of those who trespass on my land, killing my animals without permission. She pointed her elegant, branch-like finger at Robert. "You've hunted on my land before!"

He gathered his nerves to speak. "I haven't since I was a teen."

"You admit to it. I am aware she has never killed anything. I can't even smell animal meat deep in her stomach. You may go under one demand. When you two have a daughter together who reaches the age of ten, you must come back and join us forever. If you choose not to follow through, you've seen what I can do. Never speak this to anyone other than yourselves."

The men brought out their knives again. Lara and Robert understood, and they held their hands and palms forward without even being instructed. They were cut deeply, wiping it on each other's cheeks before kissing.

"The return ritual has been committed to. You will join us when it is time. Now go." Lara and Robert looked at their hands and faces. It was as if the ritual had never occurred. Abnoba didn't have to tell them more than once. They got up, holding each other, inhaling the piercing air as they returned to the cottage.

"Do you want to go home now, or should we wait until the morning?" She asked anxiously.

"We need to go back now. Let's get our stuff packed. We could get to Madison in an hour and stay at the hotel there."

"That sounds like it would be a better plan. I won't be able to sleep here."

The incredible winter woods were overshadowed by their nerves. They were lucky to leave with their lives, even at a cost. Exhausted and shaken, they drove for an hour, repeating the events. Lara and Robert were young and should have been excited about their future together.

College was hectic with their studies, her being in a fashion design program and Robert getting his BA in biology. They held down their secret and tried to move forward with graduating and planning their wedding. Even twenty years later, that experience never left them. They always remembered the promise to Abnoba, Goddess of the Forest. One day, they would have to join the deep-woods cult against their will. Maybe it was better if they were sacrificed together that night.

It was finally updated. Now, she tapped the section she wanted most. The names, cities, and contact information of her birth family, especially her parents. Her parents were Michael and Patricia Mueller, and she had four sisters and nine brothers. That hurt her a lot.

With that many kids, why was I given up, she thought.

She still believed there had to be a reason. Lara grimaced and wanted to throw up after looking at the family tree section. There was a lot of incest between members. Maybe knowing wasn't the best decision. Her adoptive parents were right that she didn't need this knowledge. She had no idea if they knew the details or not. This was a discussion for another time. Looking at the location information made sense and filled her with dread. Everyone lived in Ziigwan, the same place where they witnessed a human sacrifice many years ago and had to make a deal with evil. Something told her that this was destined to happen. The main question now was how was she given up for adoption if they wanted her so badly? Was the Goddess Abnoba just waiting for her to have a family so there would be more people to join their insane backwoods cult? Were her adoptive parents involved in this somehow? She needed to call them ASAP. It couldn't wait any longer. She picked up the phone and speed-dialed them.

"Hi, Mom, put Dad on speaker too. We need to speak."

"Okay, I will. What is this about?"

"I've always known I was adopted. Why didn't you ever tell me about my birth family? Do not lie to me!"

"Your parents were from a rural part of Wisconsin. They grew up in poverty and wanted you to live a good life, where you were safe from the awful aspects of that kind of place and people, if you know what I mean," she said.

"Yeah, I know exactly what you mean." She thought back to how incest was the least of the problems up there. Her parents had no idea what she and Robert went through that horrendous night.

"Honey, we love you. That's why we have done everything we can for you. What is this about?" her father asked.

"I did a DNA test to find out more about my birth parents and heritage. My ancestors were German immigrants who settled in Ziigwan, Wisconsin."

"Please, whatever you do, I beg you not to find them," her mother pleaded. They aren't the kind of people you want to be around. Robert should never meet them; you cannot have your daughter around them. I mean it."

"Is there something you aren't telling me, Mom?"

"Patricia, your birth mother, told me you needed to be with a family that could keep you safe."

"How did you know them? It sounds like my adoption was urgent."

"It doesn't matter, Lara. You belong to us, not them," her father said.

Lara didn't want to correct them. She and the rest of her family soon would belong to that clan and the Goddess Abnoba.

"Yes, it does matter!"

"Don't get upset. This is all in the past, and you have nothing to worry about. Yes, your adoption wasn't legal. I met Patricia and Michael at a homeless shelter in Milwaukee. Both said they escaped some kind of survivalist nature cult. That you would be in danger for the rest of your life if they remained there with you. The other children ended up in homes, too."

"So these people had the potential to find and kidnap me or even put my child in jeopardy? My siblings are all back there, not living in good, loving homes."

"It's unlikely those people would come after you. I had no idea your birth parents went back. Your siblings probably moved up there after discovering where they originally came from. It happens often."

"Okay. I love you both. I am so sorry that I bothered you. We all love you. I will have Emma talk to you once they get back from the store. They went to get supper and dessert for her birthday."

"Bye, honey. I'm sorry we didn't tell you sooner." Lara hung up. She was even more emotional than before. They lied to her all these years to protect her, but fate had its way.

"Hey, hon, we're back from the store!" Robert yelled from the door.

"We got lots of yummy things, like sushi and chocolate chip cookies!" exclaimed Emma. Those were her favorite foods, but obviously, she did not eat the two together. They dragged the bags in, setting them on the floor. Emma was the first to notice her mom crying.

"What's wrong? Why are you so sad?" she asked in a soft, comforting tone. Robert turned around after putting the last cold item in the fridge.

"Lara?" He glanced at her. Impulsively, he hugged her from behind while she was still sitting in the chair, staring at her phone. It was the first time she had actively ignored them.

"You are okay, and we love you no matter what. Now, please tell us what's going on. I know this isn't easy," he said caringly. Emma rubbed her shoulder.

"I found information that I can't say in front of our daughter," she said, struggling with each word. Her feet didn't want to work, so Robert ended up helping her to the couch in the front room.

"Emma, could you put some of your music on and read a book in your room while me and your mom talk?"

"Is this about the other mom and dad that she doesn't know?" she asked innocently.

"Yes, Mom is going through a lot, and we need privacy, okay, sweetie? Thank you."

Emma flitted to her room with a book about cats.

"I found out that I'm 100% German and my parents came from a cult and gave me up to keep me safe. They are originally from Ziigwan, Wisconsin."

Robert grew pale and called Emma over. He knew this day was coming.

Lara dialed her mom and dad again.

"Grandma and Grandpa want to say Happy Birthday."

"Hi, Grandma and Grandpa! I turned ten today!" They sang to her joyfully while Robert and Lara tried to hold their tears in.

"Bye, Grandma and Grandpa, love you!"

"Emma, dear. It's time we take a trip," Lara said sorrowfully. We must pack everything we can into the car, plus Sadie, okay?"

"I'm so excited! I love trips! Where are we going?"

"We're going to a cottage in the woods up north," Robert said.

FLESH AND BLOOD

BY DAVID K. SLATER

The doctor took out a pad and pen—that's how you know it's bad news. Anything where they need to show you a diagram is bad news. Joel Parkes sat in silence and held Debbie's hand under the desk.

The doctor said things like 'aggressive,' 'inoperable' and 'matter of months,' while Joel listened to his heartbeat as it pounded in his head like a kick-drum. Debbie wept. He couldn't turn and look at her for fear of crying himself, but he felt it. He didn't know how to comfort her. So he squeezed her hand so tightly his fingers blanched white.

After they left the office, they hugged and cried and made promises, promises that neither of them could keep. Debbie fell to pieces before Joel's eyes over the next few weeks. It was like someone letting the air out of an inflatable animal. She had disappeared so quickly, he had no time to register it. The saddest part was he spent so much time worrying about what he would do when she was gone that he didn't experience those last months. He was already clinging to a ghost before she let go.

Joel took the backseat throughout his life, and now fate had thrust the keys into his sweaty palm and said, "You drive."

Henry was his responsibility now. He'd hardly come to terms with the idea of being a father of a two parent family. Now he was a widower with no choice but to protect this beautiful boy and shape him into the best person he could. *How can you make a good person if you don't believe you're a good person yourself?*

He had his mother's eyes, her golden blonde hair, and her smile that always made Joel feel like everything would be ok. Even as memories of her face faded, Henry was a living, breathing reminder of their love. Nobody had ever made Joel feel like a real person as much as Debbie had. She would swear up and down that she didn't do anything special, but he knew different. She *was* special.

He'd never shied away from changing nappies or spending time with the boy. To tell the truth, he'd enjoyed most of the things about being a parent that had initially worried him. The real challenge was replacing a mother's touch. If Henry fell down and hurt himself, or even if he just wanted someone to comfort him as he slept, Joel was always second best. He would never have the same bond with their son that Debbie had. The lack of sleep hit him worst of all. At some point in his late twenties, Joel figured out he needed eight hours of sleep to function at anywhere close to his full potential. Anything less and his mood would sour. All that went out of the window. Grouchy was now his default setting.

His daily routine became a war of attrition between his body and his rapidly declining mental health. The fog clouded his brain for months before he lost himself. With no sleep, and a cycle of fear and regret running through his mind, The Woman first came to him.

She was five feet tall, with wiry black hair and eyes like daggers. Her top lip was as thick with hair as her forearms and she wore clothes that hadn't been washed in years. She was a walking bag of dirty laundry.

Joel stood in the middle of a busy store, trying to remember what he'd come in for. If he left the house for something without a shopping list, he almost never came home with the right thing anymore. Everything was too much for him in those places—too bright, too noisy. The racket of other people felt oppressive to him now. It would only take a few minutes before he wanted to drop his shopping basket and run. There, in the middle of the pulsating mess of *other people*; he spotted her.

"Can I hold him?" she asked with an almost sinister look on her face.

No, Joel thought. *You can't.*

Now she stood closer. He was able to take in every putrid detail of her rotten face. Thick lines ran across her forehead and down her cheeks, where filth had become caked in such deep layers that the natural lines were filled with a flaky crust. Her eyes were rat-like, bulging, black orbs that protruded from their sockets. Her face was like a Halloween mask you wouldn't buy for a child in case it scared them too much. The feel of her sour breath on Joel's skin made him take a step backward from her. She immediately advanced on him to close the gap.

Joel's social anxiety kicked in hard. *What do I do?* What does anyone do in this situation. You can read as many books on parenting as you like. None of them will tell you how to deal with a situation like this.

"Go on... Can I hold him? Pass him to me," she practically hissed.

Why isn't someone stopping this?

"I'm sorry," Joel replied. "He's due for a nap. I need to get him home."

Henry beamed up at the old bag, showing his five shiny white teeth. Drool glistened on his chin.

"Don't be daft; he's wide awake. *Give him to me.*" Her eyes met Joel's.

"No, I have to go," Joel said as he manoeuvred Henry's pushchair around her and darted for the exit. She stood in the middle of the aisle and smiled as they disappeared out of sight.

Henry had always loved his preschooler's music class. They still went once a week to shake rattles and bang on drums while a Disney store reject played guitar and sang to them. The mood of those classes was like a day care for the mentally ill. *This is being a parent*, Joel thought—pretending to enjoy something that verged on torture for him. Halfway through the class, he sensed something wasn't right. Like someone was pulling at the hairs on the back of his neck. Something primal awakened within him. Then his blood turned to ice as he saw her face. *She's at the window.*

It was only for a moment. Perhaps she hadn't been there at all. That seemed more likely. *I'm losing my mind,* he thought.

Then she appeared at the playground.

Henry played in the sandpit with the other kids his age. Joel sat on the bench opposite, idly scrolling through his phone and wondering how long he had to wait before he could leave and still think of himself as a good parent. *Twenty minutes, is twenty minutes enough?* He glanced up from the screen and saw her standing just outside the surrounding fence. Her stance opened wide and her hands hung at her sides like a gunslinger. She grinned from ear to ear.

Joel looked around to see if any of the other parents noticed this human rag-doll who stood before them. Her hands now raised to clutch at the fence.

He snatched Henry up from the pit and turned his back on that vile woman. He marched as fast as he could and headed home. Just to make sure she didn't follow them, he went the long way back.

Every day beyond that, Joel experienced a mixture of dread, loneliness, and guilt. Despite having to spend every waking hour with his son, Joel felt like the last man on earth. He talked to nobody, had nobody to tell him what to do.

Joel never believed in fate, or anything of that nature. A friend once asked him, "Do you believe in the universe?" He'd laughed at that question. It was so broad and empty, so filled with directionless hope that it had to be a joke. No, there was nothing more to life. Life itself was enough. Joel stood in line at a supermarket, pondering the vast emptiness of the universe, when an old Gypsy woman took his arm.

"Hey," she said, "fancy running into you here. I've just got my last lucky bit of heather. This is meant for you, so I'll let you have it cheap. Five pounds."

Through narrowed eyes, Joel judged the woman. *This seems like bullshit. Maybe I could use some bullshit, though,* he thought. Then his core beliefs managed to override the circus currently running in his mind. "No thanks," he said without making eye contact.

"Suit yourself," she replied and turned away.

"Wait..." he blurted out. "Can you read my fortune?"

Now the Gypsy woman narrowed her eyes.

"Uhh, sure. Twenty quid."

She took him by the hand and led him away from the queue. They stood in the middle of a supermarket aisle, just between the dog food and the bird feeders.

"Show me your hand." She grabbed his arm, flipping his palm skyward. "Oh, and the twenty."

With his free hand, Joel reached into his pocket and pulled out a crumpled twenty pound note. She took it from him without taking her eyes off his upturned hand.

"Hmmm, very interesting. You've suffered a loss. You're looking for answers..."

Well, duh. Joel thought, already feeling the loss of his wasted money.

Then the strangest thing happened. In the middle of a crowded supermarket, everything around them seemed to drop into soft focus. The other people in the store slowed almost to a standstill. The Gypsy woman's eyes lit up.

"Tomorrow is promised for no man, live for today," she spoke.

What is that supposed to mean?

With that, the world around them resumed normality. Joel shook his head, like he had just woken from a dream.

"Nice doing business with you. Look after that boy." She smiled.

"Thanks, I'll do my best."

Later that night, Joel couldn't help but think about what the Gypsy woman had said. Visions of the last six months swirled in his head. Throughout all the movies he saw in the back of his mind, one theme prevailed—loneliness and fear. *What kind of life was that?*

It came time to shut off the lights and lay down in bed for another night of restless sleep. From upstairs, Joel heard a gentle crackling sound. He hadn't left the TV on; he felt sure of that. He couldn't even watch TV anymore. All of his favourite shows reminded him of Debbie. How could he laugh at the jokes on screen without her? The dead voices of the canned laughter only served to remind him of how empty a memory can be. People spend all of their lives making memories. Moments with loved ones to cherish forever. The cold truth is, when that person you love dies, those memories become little more than two-dimensional images that fade with each passing year. You can kid yourself that you feel the afterglow of that love, but with nobody there to reciprocate, it's an exercise in futility. First you forget them, then someone else forgets you. That is the nature of things.

Tiptoeing upstairs, Joel listened intently, sifting for more details in the sound like a gold prospector. At the top of the landing, he saw the bathroom door stood ajar. In the darkened room, he could just make out a sliver of the far side wall. The white tiles seemed to be faintly illuminated by a pale blue flickering light. With bated breath, Joel continued closer to the door, as the light on the tiles shimmered and switched occasionally, as though someone flicked channels on a detuned television set.

Should I speak? Would I even want to hear a reply if I did?

Somewhere woven into the static hiss was the sound of several different news readers. Each one from a different city, or different country. All the news was bad. Death, mayhem, murder.

His feet continued their same mechanical onward trajectory. There was no other outcome here. He would find out what waited in the shadows for him.

Joel reached out with a trembling hand and pushed the door open, stepping into the bathroom, still unable to speak. He silently marched toward whatever was hiding in the shadows. As Joel crossed the threshold to the bathroom, the lights stopped. The dark embraced him like an old friend.

It took a long while for Joel to convince himself that nothing had happened.

You're just tired.

He hugged Henry tightly before putting him in his cot. After turning on the elephant shaped nightlight, Joel walked across the room to shut the curtains. With no particular motive, he opened the curtains, just a crack, and looked outside.

There she stood. Right on the front lawn. Their eyes locked in an instant. Joel froze on the spot, unable to even move his hand the few inches needed to close the curtain.

Suddenly, she bolted across the front garden and towards the house. He would never have guessed that she could move so fast..

Did I lock the doors?

He hardly had time to finish the thought before an aggressive knocking started at the front door. The rhythm boomed through the door, too fast for a human hand, and without breaks, like a record playing over and over, relentlessly.

"Go away!" He was surprised to hear himself yell.

The knocking stopped as suddenly as it began. A sigh of relief crept to the back of Joel's throat, but didn't dare make its exit.

Every door, every window, everything that wasn't nailed down; shook and rattled in unison, Henry wailed in his cot.

Too afraid to move, Joel sat with his knees pulled up to his chest and sobbed.

I don't know what to do. I don't know what to do.

The alarm clock went off at six am, but Joel hadn't slept. His bloodshot eyes had all but dried out as he laid on his bed, staring that the ceiling.

"Go, we have to leave this place. Get up. Get up!" He willed himself.

In a matter of minutes, he threw bags in the car, strapped Henry in his seat and hit the road. In the rear-view mirror, he caught a glimpse of The Woman standing on the front lawn as they sped away.

She was at every traffic light and every crowded bus stop. He couldn't escape her, no matter how quickly he sped through the busy streets. Eventually they left the city, and it wasn't long before she was every scarecrow, standing alone in every field.

The petrol tank was almost empty as Joel rolled into the seaside town of Scarborough. He felt like he hadn't eaten in days and the smell in the car told him that Henry needed his nappy changed as soon as possible. They pulled up to a busy-looking chain pub, the kind where the food, the service, and the beers were all dependably crappy.

Joel ordered a meal and asked for the baby changing room. A ratty looking man with a ponytail that clung on for dear life pointed him in the right direction. Joel felt relief wash over him as he found the room and shut the door behind him, blocking out some of the noise of the busy pub. He laid Henry on the baby changing mat and took out a clean nappy.

"Come on then, son," Joel smiled. "Let's get your bum changed."

Henry smiled up at him, in the way he always did. So happy for someone to be interacting with him. Truth be told, Henry was such a good kid. He beamed at anyone who made eye contact with him. Something had changed recently though—something more in that look of recognition when he would first see his dad in the morning or even if he'd just left the room for a minute. Trust, maybe even love.

They quickly returned to their table as the food arrived. Joel glanced around the busy pub at all the other people, day drinking, or stopping in for a quick bite to eat before spending the rest of their day in the arcades.

How did it all go so wrong?

This thought landed like someone whispering in Joel's ear. Then he realised this feeling wasn't his own. He looked at Henry smiling back at him from the highchair. The kid chewed on a rusk, getting more in his hair than his mouth. Joel thought to himself, I'm lucky to have the chance to take care of this boy. I have a purpose in life. That's enough; and with that, he took a life affirming bite of his three ninety-nine burger.

Then he saw her.

Smiling from across the crowded room.

Everyone in the bar fell silent. They turned their heads in unison and stared at Joel and Henry. *They're all in on it!*

With a slow jerky movement as though she were on rails, The Woman glided towards them, through the now deathly silent room.

Although she was far beyond Joel's reach, he heard and felt her rasping breath in his ear. Felt it on his neck.

Joel screamed. Frozen in place, like he was tied to his seat, he screamed and he waited for her to come and take his son from him.

In the blink of an eye she was gone, but every one of the bar's patrons still looked at him, horror now filling their eyes.

Am I still screaming?

Hurriedly, he grabbed Henry from his highchair, leaving a room of shocked people in their wake.

"I'm not crazy. I promise you I am not crazy," he muttered as he fled.

Joel dashed from the pub with Henry in his arms. They passed the busy seafront arcades. The smell of hot dogs and candy floss was thick in the sea salt air. He left everything else behind and clutched his boy tightly to his chest.

In the blink of an eye, he was running on the beach, parallel to the sea. The wet sand sucking at his feet. Seagulls cried out in the distance as the fairground music of the arcade blared on.

By some coincidence, Joel spotted an unattended row boat by the shore. He jumped into it and after placing Henry down gently, he started rowing.

She can't follow me out here.

Without consideration for his safety, Joel rowed as fast as he could, propelling the boat towards the horizon. The sun started its agonising descent.

From the pier he saw The Woman glaring at them, teeth still bared in some sinister attempt at a smile. Her face was as empty as an unmanned ventriloquist doll.

Joel continued onwards, heading for the setting sun like the light at the end of a sewer tunnel. Rain fell and a cold wind started to blow.

Minutes or hours could have passed as Joel tried in vain to put distance between himself and that foul creature on the pier. He felt a flash of light from behind him. Like lightning, only without the definition. This was more like someone turning a light on, a second sun.

He glanced over his shoulder and saw something that drained the air from his lungs and made his stomach clench like a fist.

There was a crack in the sky, and hands reached down to him—reaching down for Henry.

Tears ran down Joel's face as he looked into the light beyond the arms, which were as cold and solid as granite. There was something warm and wonderful just behind the clinical glare which spewed from the hole in the sky. Cold fire. More arms forced their way through the jagged tear in our universe and lunged toward the tiny boat. Rain continued to fall on either side of them, but somehow Joel and Henry remained dry.

Joel averted his eyes from the horror above and looked down at his son.

Henry smiled at him with the innocence of youth, Debbie's smile.

Time seemed to stop for a moment, where even the rain refused to fall.

Maybe we can create a moment that won't be forgotten.

Joel turned his back on Henry and screamed up at the bleeding sky.

"Take me!"

Hands reached into his chest, crushing and ripping out his heart in one motion. They dragged him toward the blinding light. The tears on his face boiled and evaporated under the scorching heat. More and more arms burst from the opening. They snatched and clawed at his body like stray dogs fighting over a chicken carcass.

Somewhere in the pain and the horror, Joel felt a single hand reach out and stroke his cheek.

With a deafening sound, like the fabric of time being torn in reverse, the rift closed up and all that remained was a glowing scar across a darkening sky.

Joel was gone.

The rain stopped.

The water settled.

And his boy was left alone, adrift on an ocean of uncertainty.

Henry smiled up at the twinkling stars, memories of his father's love already beginning to fade, as the waves gently rocked him to sleep.

NUGGET

BY JYL GLENN

Ellen pulled off the highway, exhausted. She was late getting to her conference, but she was out of gas in every sense imaginable. Ellen followed the road signs telling her there was a Love's truck stop two miles away. She could see the big lighted sign in the sky ahead, but when she pulled into the parking lot—the store was in complete darkness. She pulled up to the gas pumps, hoping she could pay with a card, but found those were not working either.

"Closed! Are you fucking kidding me!?" she yelled and pounded the steering wheel in frustration.

Just to the left of the Love's sat a motel. *Well, at least the lights are on,* she thought as she drove across the parking lot toward the motel.

When she got a little closer, she rolled her eyes at the motel's name.

"Cadillac Motel, seriously?" she muttered. She turned the car off and stepped out. The neon "Vacancy" sign was lit and buzzed faintly in the damp evening air, while the "FREE HBO" sign right below was missing the letter B.

"Free HO!" She couldn't help but laugh. *In a place like this, that tracks.*

Ellen sighed, resigning herself to her fate. "Well, I guess it's this or I sleep in my car in a parking lot in East Bumfuck. Cool, cool, cool."

She trudged toward the office, her shoes crunching on the gravel parking lot. As she approached, she noticed the peeling paint on the building's exterior and the cobwebs adorning the corners of the windows. The place looked like it hadn't seen a renovation since the Reagan administration. She pushed the creaky door open and was slapped with the smell of mothballs, yesterday's burnt coffee, and stale cigarettes.

Inside, the lobby was dimly lit, the front desk abandoned. Ellen rang the bell a few times before a figure popped their head out from around a curtain behind the counter, startling her. She let out a small yelp and stumbled backward.

"Welcome to the Cadillac Motel," croaked an elderly man with wild, unkempt hair, and thick glasses that magnified his eyes to an unsettling degree. "My name is Walter. Do you need a room for the night?"

Ellen caught her breath, her heart still racing from the surprise. "Uh, yeah. Just one night. I ran out of gas and the truck stop is closed."

The old man nodded slowly, his oversized eyes never blinking. "We don't get many visitors these days. You're in luck, though. We have plenty of vacancies and they should open back up around seven tomorrow morning."

The old man reached for a dusty ledger. "Name?"

"Ellen," she replied, glancing around the lobby. Faded pictures of old cars hung crookedly on the walls, and a stuffed

raccoon posed menacingly on a shelf behind the desk. "Nice...
decor," she added sarcastically.

The old man raised an eyebrow at her comment, scribbling
in the ledger with a shaky hand. "That'll be forty-five dollars.
Cash only. And that *'decor'* is my old pet raccoon, Nugget.
Best dog I ever had!" Walter expelled a half wheeze, half laugh.
"That'll be fifty dollars, now."

"Of course." She rifled through her purse , a bit
embarrassed, and handed him some cash.

"Room 13," he said, holding out the key. "It's our best
room."

"Room 13, huh? How lucky for me," she said with a
forced smile. "I don't suppose you have a vending machine or
anything? I'm starving."

The old man's magnified eyes seemed to bore into her. "No
vending machines. But there's a mini-fridge in your room. We
try to keep some snacks stocked for our late-night arrivals.
Help yourself to whatever's inside. No extra charge."

Ellen nodded; not entirely sure she wanted to see the
contents of a mini-fridge in this place. "Great, thanks. And,
uh, which way is room 13?"

"Outside, to your left. End of the row. Nice quiet spot,
the furthest room from that noisy truck stop," the old man
replied, his gaze never wavering.

Ellen stepped outside and headed toward her room. As Ellen
passed each door, she glanced at the numbers scrawled on the
faded plaques.

7, 8, 10, 11, 12.

Odd, she thought. *No room 9? Well, it's no surprise these
people can't count.*

With a bit of wiggling and jiggling of the key in the
doorknob, she got her room open and stepped inside. She

couldn't shake the feeling that this place was holding its breath. The walls were covered in faded floral wallpaper, and the floorboards creaked beneath her as she walked. It smelled of stale air, thick with dust, and something more...intangible. The space was small, and very sparsely furnished with a bed, a TV, and a single chair by the window. Flashes of the neon sign in the parking lot peeked in through the gaps in the drawn curtains. She tossed her bag on the bed and made her way to the bathroom. The mirror was cracked, and the light flickered overhead. Naturally, Psycho came to mind, and she flung the shower curtain back as fast as she could to make sure there wasn't a killer lying in wait for their next victim.

She let out a laugh. "Of course it's empty, you idiot," she said.

She turned back to the sink and turned the water on to rinse her face. She looked in the cracked mirror, her face fragmented by the crack and sighed. "Girl, you should have stopped for the night hours ago in a real city, this place is a dump," she scolded herself. Ellen leaned forward to splash some water on her face. She stood back up and looked at herself in the mirror again, and noticed something in the reflection. For a brief second, she swore she saw a figure standing just behind her—a woman, thin, with hollow, dark eyes and an empty smile.

She whirled around, but the bathroom was empty.

Just the shadows, she told herself, wiping her face with her hands. *It's just the shadows. Too much windshield time today. Get it together. God, I hate it here.*

Ellen stepped out of the bathroom to get her essentials unpacked for the night. She knew she had seen a small closet when she walked in, the kind with those ugly louvered bi-fold doors, but it would have to do. She needed to hang up her clothes for the next day, so she was at least somewhat presentable if she ever made it to her conference.

Ellen reached for the closet door, her hand hesitating for a moment before grasping the little wooden knob. As she pulled it open, she expected to see a small, dusty space with some cobwebs and hopefully a few wire hangers. Instead, she found herself staring into another room. She closed the door, shook her head, and then opened it again.

"No way!"

She was taken aback as she took in the scene before her. The room was identical to hers, but everything was backward, like a mirror image. The bed was on the opposite side; the chair faced the other direction, and even the lumps and tears in the wallpaper seemed to be a mirror image of her room.

"What the hell?" she whispered, her voice barely audible.

She stepped closer to the threshold, peering into the strange duplicate room. The air felt colder here, and she could swear she heard faint whispers coming from somewhere inside. Her heart raced as she debated whether to step through or slam the door shut.

Curious, Ellen stepped forward, her fingers brushing the cool surface of the faded floral wallpaper on the walls. There was something wrong with the air. It felt heavier here, like a thick fog pressing in on her chest. She took another tentative step into the room and heard a loud bang behind her.

She jumped. "What the ever-loving fuck!" *Those cheap ass doors shouldn't be able to slam.* But when she turned around, it was...a wall, covered in more of the same old, ugly floral wallpaper.

Ellen's heart raced as she frantically ran her hands over the wallpaper, searching for any sign of a door or seam. But there was nothing—just an unbroken expanse of faded flowers.

"No, no, no," she muttered, her voice rising with panic. "Nope! This isn't happening. This can't be happening."

She spun around, taking in the mirror image of her original room. Everything was the same, yet subtly wrong. Ellen stumbled to the window; yanking open the curtains. Instead of the parking lot and neon sign, she saw only an inky blackness that seemed to swallow all the light. She pressed her face against the glass, trying to make out any shapes or movement, but there was nothing. She went to the door of the room to leave and go explain what happened to the old man at the front desk. There was no doorknob, no hinges, and only the faintest outline of where the seam should have been. The door had a peephole and one of those "you are here" maps that should have emergency exit instructions. It read:

Room 9. No Exit. Love, Nugget.

"Well...fuck me. Nugget! That goddamn taxidermy raccoon!? What kind of sick joke is this?" she yelled.

She raced to the bathroom to see if there was a window but stopped short, thinking back to checking the shower in the other room. She stopped halfway over the threshold and crept to the shower and took a deep breath. *Not today, Norman,* she thought, as she whipped the shower curtain open as quickly as she could.

Behind the curtain stood...nothing. Empty as a drum. But there was no window. She should have known better. *There must be some way out of here.* Defeated, she went back into the hotel room. *Fine, I'll just smash the front window out.* She grabbed the chair and swung it with everything she had, hoping to shatter the glass.

The chair struck the window, and the glass stretched.

"What the..." she said with utter confusion.

The window glass has stretched, like some sort of industrial strength Saran Wrap. Before she could wrap her brain around that little mind-fuck, there was a sudden knock at the door.

"HELP!!" she screamed as loud as she could. "You have to get me out of here! Hello? Hello!? Can you hear me?"

The pounding continued.

"I can't open the door, dammit! You'll have to open it from your side." She heard no response. The knocking quit for a moment and then turned to what sounded like scratching.

"Hello?" she whimpered. She stepped up to the door to look out the peephole and saw Walter, the old man from the front desk.

He stood outside, holding and stroking that disgusting raccoon, Nugget, from the lobby. He smiled. And then his smile grew wider...and wider.

Behind her, she heard the shower curtain slide along the rod. She spun around and saw the woman she thought she had seen earlier. Her face was gaunt, with hollow eyes that bored into her with a chilling blackness. Somehow, Walter's voice came from the woman and said, "Nugget doesn't like entitled bitches, unless he's hungry."

"No, no, no! Fuck off! Let me OUT!"

She turned back to the door and started pounding on it. "Let me out!" She looked through the peephole again and all she saw was one large, magnified eyeball staring back at her. The walls started closing in on her and she felt a papery hand brush the back of her neck. She pivoted slowly and came face-to-face with the woman, and with Walter with his too big eyes, holding his feral, salivating raccoon.

Ellen screamed.

The next morning, when Kat arrived to relieve Walter, the parking lot was empty as usual.

"Good morning, Walt. No guests last night?"

"No, ma'am."

"How do you afford to keep this place open?"

"Ahhh, you let me worry about that, missy. You have a good day, and if anyone shows up..."

"I know. Room 13 is our best room. Go get some sleep, old man. I'll see you tonight."

Walter shuffled away, and the motel stood unchanged, as it always had, waiting for its next visitor.

SHOPPING FOR THE HOMELESS

BY JACINTA RAE

Jeremy watched his wife nervously twirl a strand of blonde curls around her finger as they stopped at the traffic light next to the shopping plaza.

"Would you relax, please? You know the routine and that's exactly how it must look. Just breathe and follow my lead and everything will be fine," he reassured her the best he could, while his own heart pounded in overdrive.

"What if she's not there tonight?" Shelby asked.

Jeremy reached over and squeezed his wife's hand. "She'll be there. And if she's not, then there is always next week. I don't know why you are so worried. It's not like this is our first time."

The packed parking lot was starting to empty out and the sole lamp post flickered, like it had for the last two months. The building was sectioned into four stores, with three of them out of business for over two years. The one remaining shop, Teddy's Market, was the only grocery store for miles.

They kept the landlord happy, and the plaza remained active on their business alone.

At one time, southern Vermont was quaint, with its horse and carriages and Victorian style homes. The homes still stood, but the quaintness faded after decades of greed and poverty. Devastation was everywhere now. Its nimble fingers wrapped around the weak and vulnerable, choking the life out of them until one day they could not even recognize their own reflection. Needles were as common as leaves when walking the back roads and people who normally wouldn't give you the time of day came out like cockroaches in the night, begging for anything you could drop their way. Sores covered them like measles and bones protruded from their sad wasted lives. The government turned the local hotels into housing units for the homeless and the ambulance was a frequent visitor, retrieving overdose victims at least once a day.

They got out of the vehicle and grabbed their shopping bags like every Thursday night when they went grocery shopping. Consistency was important. The clerk greeted them with an empty smile as they walked through the store, filling their cart with all the basic essentials needed, like milk, bread, peanut butter, bleach, and duct tape.

Excitement and nervousness brushed over Jeremy when they were leaving the store and getting back into his dad's old red Ford Bronco that had been sitting in the garage for years. They only drove it when they went grocery shopping so as not to attract attention to any of their friends if they were spotted. No one would ever expect to see them in anything but their shiny new BMWs. Small towns had a way of knowing everyone's business and it was already risky enough planning this five minutes from their house—but last time went so smoothly.

On cue, their rag-doll came into view. Long, scraggly, bleached orange hair ran down her back. Her clothes barely covered what meat she had left on her and her small breasts hung out the sides of her tattered shirt. A row of overgrown purple hydrangea bushes partially hid their view as they watched her walk across the parking lot toward her boyfriend, who stood beside the stop sign. The tall young man, who barely weighed more than the cardboard sign that he held, bent down when he saw his girlfriend coming toward him. He gathered his bags of food that were donated to him earlier by a few generous customers who shopped at the market. He met her under the covered canopy that was used for returning the shopping carts. Words were exchanged as he handed her the sign that read, "Homeless and Hungry. Please help!" After a few minutes of chatting, they kissed and parted ways.

Jeremy and Shelby waited until she got situated in her office by the stop sign, where she and her boyfriend tagged-teamed the innocent. His shift ended at six o'clock while hers just began. Later they would meet up for their game of *Find the Vein* while their supporters were at home tucking their children to sleep and planning their next scheduled workday.

Slowly, Jeremy drove the vehicle out of its spot and waited until all the cars had pulled out onto the main road before moving forward. He watched her big brown eyes light up when she saw the familiar Bronco approaching from the distance. Haley stood next to the road and awaited her weekly, pre-made Italian submarine that got handed to her through the driver's window, which sometimes came with a side of small chit chat.

"Hey Haley, how's it going?" Jeremy asked, handing her the sandwich. "It's supposed to get chilly tonight. Do you have any warmer clothes with you?" Even though his thoughts were far from covering her tiny torso.

"Hi, guys. Yeah, I might have forgotten to pack them," Haley answered and threw her hands up in the air to mimic her fictitious story.

Jeremy eyed her half shirt as it rose higher, exposing the bottoms of her perky tits. From the first time they spotted her begging, he knew she was the one. It was the way she smiled at every passing car. Even when they gave her nothing, she still expelled a sweet juiciness he couldn't wait to taste.

Shelby nudged her husband's leg when she saw his hypnotized state of mind lingering too long on Haley's skin and decided to intervene on his behalf.

"I have a jacket in the back, if you're interested. You can keep it. It's too small for me," Shelby said.

Jeremy glanced at his wife and smiled. She normally let him do the talking, which was the way he liked it, but her offering tonight helped to wave off any red flags.

A gust of wind whipped by and knocked the sign out of Haley's hands. She ran to catch it before it went into the street, and that's when Jeremy opened his door and offered to get it for her.

Shelby was already opening the back door to grab the jacket for Haley when Jeremy returned. He walked past Haley to the rear, where his wife stood and motioned for Haley to come over as well.

Haley was cold, and she needed her sign back, so she followed his command. Normally, she would never get that close to any stranger's car. She knew the rules, but she also knew the Sawyers, and they were a nice, middle-aged Christian couple who loved to help their community. At least that's what they told her over their last few conversations. They both stood average height with blonde curls, which in turn made them look more like siblings rather than husband and wife. Their mannerism was their selling point. They fed her and genuinely seem to care about her well-being. Most people gave her nasty looks, but they never did, and she respected them for that.

Haley stood beside Shelby and peered over her shoulder as she rifled through a duffel bag. The back seat revealed the bags of groceries that were previously purchased, including the duct tape which laid on top. Her breathing sped up when she felt Jeremy's torso lean up against her back. His hands wrapped around her hips as he pulled himself closer to get a better look in the vehicle. Uncomfortable, Haley swiftly moved out from his grasp, while her sympathetic nervous system went into fight-or-flight mode. She began walking back toward the parking lot without the jacket or her sign—she could make another sign, and she had her added adrenaline keeping her warm.

Shelby's head promptly popped out from the back seat, with a blue denim jacket in hand, and said, "Found it!"

Embarrassed by her quick reaction to Jeremy's embrace, Haley turned back around to apologize and was surprisingly met face to face. Their eyes locked, and he raised his hand and covered her mouth with a damp cloth.

Haley awoke to the buzzing of a dryer announcing its completion. The smell of bleach filled the air, and her head throbbed. The familiar narration of a television commercial for cat treats played in the distance. Haley's mind pictured the tabby cat jumping in the air. Her memory went back to the parking lot and losing her sign, then...oh yeah, getting chloroformed.

Laughter erupted from above, and she recognized Jeremy's deep voice. She focused on her surroundings and concluded that she was in the unfinished basement of her kidnappers. Pipes stretched across the ceiling with puffs of pink insulation poking out in between. There were two basement hopper windows on opposite sides of the room that brought in a dim light which radiated from the full moon and starry sky. A combination lock held together chains that were wrapped around Haley's wrists. She kicked her feet apart to make sure she was not bound to any other object and concluded that she was free to walk. The mattress under her was made with soft sheets and fluffy pillows for her comfort, and there was a small television on a table in front of her with an old VCR player which rested atop. She also noticed a 35mm camera sitting on a tripod in the far corner, pointing in her direction. Her surroundings were all too familiar and panic sank in quickly. *I already survived this. How can it be happening again?*

A door opened at the top of the stairs, and Haley saw Shelby and Jeremy standing there smiling with a laundry basket at their feet.

"Oh good, you're awake, and just in time to help with the laundry," she heard the deep voice speak.

Haley sat dumbfounded on the mattress, staring back in disbelief. Sadness filled her heart as she thought of her boyfriend, Troy. Just last night, they had talked about getting married and saving enough money to take the train to New York, where his family lived. Recent phone calls relayed his father's passing and the mention of his little sister's asking for their brother to come home struck Troy hard. He said they could start a new life, and his uncle on his mom's side would help them get jobs while they lived with his mom and sisters.

He's going to think I left him, she thought to herself as a tear trickled down her cheek.

The laundry basket came flying down the stairs, jolting Haley back to her confined surroundings.

"First we clean, then we play," Jeremy said in a stern voice that made Haley take notice. "Not my words, but rules are rules."

He gave his wife an obedient wink, allowing her to proceed.

Shelby smiled at Jeremy. "And make sure to fold neatly, or I will just have you fold them again," she added.

"Help! Help me, please!" Haley screamed at the top of her lungs.

Shelby furrowed her brows at the screeching racket and disclosed, "Nobody can hear you, and you should put that energy toward getting the laundry done. I don't want to have to tell you again," she warned and slammed the basement door.

Hours were merely minutes for Haley as she struggled to break out of the lock and chains which constrained her wrists. Fortunately, the combination dial was within reach of her fingertips, but randomly turning it in different directions did not solve her dilemma. She tried wiggling her wrists out of the chains, but that proved to be painful and bloody. The mixture of her dry mouth from screaming and the blood made her stomach churn. Saliva formed in her mouth, giving her a few quenching swallows before she hurled chunks of hot dog that had been purchased earlier from a food cart on the side of the road.

Hopelessness sank in, and Haley searched desperately for an escape. She spotted the windows again and wondered if she would be able to get her body through the small frame. One of the windows rested above the clothes dryer and that seemed to be her only exit, other than the door at the top of the stairs. Haley rushed over to the dryer and climbed up. The metal top made a hollow, thumping sound as it flexed under her weight. She moved her feet to the more durable edge and tip-toed to reach the handle on the window. She gave the handle a hard turn, and it didn't budge. Again, she used all her strength to force the window open, and she slipped in the process. Her knees buckled, and she landed hard on top of the dryer, making a crashing sound that she was sure her captors he ard.

Light poured into the basement when the door opened, and Jeremy observed Haley crouched next to the untouched laundry basket.

"She didn't do the laundry, honey. Is it my turn yet?" Jeremy asked.

"Not yet," Shelby replied.

Shelby walked over and handed her husband an object, and they both giggled when they put their hands behind their back and descended the staircase.

Jeremy stood in front of Haley, smirking. "Pick one?" he asked.

"What?" was all Haley managed to spill out.

"Pick one, you stupid bitch! Me or him?" Shelby interrupted.

Taken aback by the scornful tone that had once been so kind, Haley immediately responded, "Him!"

Shelby shook her head in disappointment and pulled her hands out to reveal a thick black dog collar. She walked over and fastened the collar around Haley's neck, then pulled out a miniature key and locked it. Haley knew then that this was no ordinary dog collar.

Shelby patted Haley on the head as she walked away, saying, "Good girl."

"Wow, she didn't even fight. Much easier than Cassie, that's for sure," Jeremy stated, unveiling a remote control.

Haley stared at the controller and pieced together what was about to happen to her. She realized it didn't matter whom she picked—they were both fucking lunatics.

A shock of electricity jolted through Haley, and muttered screams erupted from her thrashing body. The smell of piss filled the air, and Shelby quickly snatched the remote out of Jeremy's hands.

Rage enveloped Shelby's face as she sniffed the stench in the room. Jeremy hung his head in remorse, awaiting his wife's wrath. Shelby poked Jeremy's side with her index finger and said, "We talked about being more patient, babe. Remember?"

Jeremey looked up at his wife and shrugged his shoulders. "I'm sorry. I just wanted to play."

Haley laid on the mattress, soiled in her own urine. Uncontrollable sobs wept from her overstimulated body while she listened to the craziness that was unfolding before her. The voices grew faint as she mentally distanced herself to her safe place—a sunny beach on a deserted island. Even though she had never seen the ocean in person, she would imagine how the ocean sounded as the waves tumbled onto the grainy sand. One lonely seagull stood along the shoreline in search of the smallest nibble of food. And the smell, she read somewhere, was consistent with algae and dead fish, but she preferred salty and fresh. A place where peace resonated in every living, breathing cell—a place where time stood still.

"Are you in there? I'm talking to you, girl," Shelby asked as she slapped Haley's face.

Haley flinched away before Shelby could get in a second slap, which made Shelby grin. She threw the basket at Haley's face and ordered, "Clean up your filth, and I would advise you to eat whatever you threw up over there, because that is all you are going to eat tonight. You disgust me!"

The light faded from the room as the door closed. Haley curled her knees up to her chest and cried, while her nerve endings found their way back to normalcy.

Footsteps thumped from up above, and Haley couldn't tell how long, or even if she had slept. At least the last time she knew her stepfather's intentions, and that was to make money. He had a "collective" group of friends that he charged per visit. Sometimes they got the group discount. His only requirement was that they weren't allowed to leave any physical evidence behind, such as bruises or semen. After five years of torture, she ran away on her sixteenth birthday. She never returned and nobody ever came looking for her. She met her boyfriend, Troy, at a train station six months later, and followed him to Vermont, where they currently lived at the Quality Inn hotel. Haley had no idea what the Sawyers had planned for her, if that was even their real last name.

"Rise and shine, gutter girl," Shelby shouted, as she descended the stairwell. "We have a busy day, and you need to eat breakfast first." Shelby's eyes scanned the room, and she immediately dropped the plate of eggs and yanked Haley up by her hair, dragging her upstairs and out the front door. Shelby threw her on the grass and grabbed the garden hose, and turned it on full blast at Haley until she was completely soaked. "I warned you not to make me tell you again, didn't I? Now get up and grab that shovel and wheelbarrow and follow me." Shelby stared at Haley with a cautioned look—daring her to disobey orders again.

Haley shivered as she got off the ground and Jeremy stood by the barn watching his wife play with their new pet.

"I have an idea," Jeremy announced. "Let's play *Naked Chicken*."

Shelby laughed at her husband. "You and your games," she said. "Fine, we can play, but I'd really like to have all this finished by lunch, and I was hoping to get the floors cleaned today as well." She turned to Haley and commanded her to strip. "You heard the man, off with your clothes. Or am I going to have to do that for you, too?"

Haley removed her wet clothes the best she could with her hands still chained. She had hoped the water from the hose destroyed any chance of getting zapped again, but she wasn't taking any chances. A quick glance at the premises showed no signs of neighbors. The woods encircled them, and no traffic could be heard, which made Haley think it went for miles.

They have no idea who they are fucking with, Haley repeated over and over to herself, doing her best to pump herself full of courage before they did God knows what to her.

Shelby spotted Haley's desperation and pointed towards the huge hill of compost by the wood line and said, "I wouldn't bother looking for help. The only people around here are the dead ones. Now, grab that shovel and clean the chicken coop, and when I say clean, I mean spotless. I want all that shit scrubbed off the walls and new bedding put down."

"Eh, um," Jeremy interrupted.

"Oh, yeah. You must cluck as you clean—it's part of the game," she winked.

Haley stood there, dumbfounded. "You want me to clean your chicken coop?" she finally asked.

"And cluck," Jeremy added.

Shelby kicked Haley in the direction of the coop. "Do you have brain damage from all those drugs you've taken, or what? If you don't want to be hosed down again, then I would suggest you start shoveling."

Haley grabbed the farming tools and did what she was told. All the years of abuse she'd suffered, this was definitely a first, she thought to herself, as she humiliatingly clucked for her spectators.

Hunger pangs overcame Haley as she finished cleaning the poop water bucket. She has slept in worse conditions than a hen house and eaten out of plenty of trash cans, so this was a walk in the park for her. Shelby wasn't the one who terrified Haley, it was her sick and twisted husband that frightened her the most. *What were his arrangements for her? And whatever happened to the last girl they had mentioned.*

Jeremy's mouth gaped open at the sight of her naked body. He slid his hand down his pants to re-adjust himself as he sat in his chair, gawking with the remote in the other hand, waiting for any reason to transport her to her knees. The front door of the house opened, and Shelby walked over with three sandwiches, one for each of them. Haley scarfed down her peanut butter and jelly before they had a chance to change their minds. She needed fuel if she was ever going to survive this absurdness.

Shelby looked at her husband and said, "I have a surprise for you. You can have her for the afternoon, but I still need the floors cleaned, so don't get carried away, okay?"

Jeremy almost choked on his last bite of sandwich when he heard his wife's words. "You got it, babe," he gleefully answered. He eyed Haley's body up and down, raised the remote in his hand, and with a lick of his tongue across his lips, he whispered, "Follow me, my sweetness."

They were heading back into the house, and Haley's visions of escaping diminished. Who was she kidding anyhow? As long as they had that remote control, she was powerless. Her only hope was to get far enough away that the connection was lost. Then maybe she'd have a chance. For now, she found it best to comply—that is something she knew how to do. Haley followed Jeremy back into the dungeon of hell, while Shelby followed momentarily with a handful of dark towels.

"Please let me go. I'll do anything you want—you don't have to hurt me. You can have sex with me. I won't fight you, I promise. I'll suck your dick and clean your toilets, or whatever the fuck it is that you want me to do. Please, I'm a good person. I don't deserve this."

Shelby laughed at Haley's request. "Good girls don't do drugs," she said.

"Not all homeless people use drugs, lady. Sometimes it's just bad fucking luck that we have no place to live," Haley sneered back.

Shelby shockingly agreed after scanning Haley's skin for needle marks and sores. "Hmm, it seems we snagged a clean one, babe."

Jeremy snorted. "She's not going to be so clean when I'm finished with her." They both laughed. Haley whimpered.

Shelby pointed to them both as she left. "You two have fun now. I'm going to go make supper. I will need her back by five o'clock, and remember, I need her arms and legs working, please."

Jeremy gave his wife a thumbs up signal and sighed heavily when he heard the basement door shut. Haley stood naked, shaking, but this time with fear. "What did she mean by that?" she tearfully asked, not sure if she wanted the answer.

Jeremy placed the towels on the ground under a skinny pipe that ran the length of the basement ceiling. He grabbed Haley's chained wrists and pulled them above her head, then attached them to a rope he had thrown over the piping. He proceeded to give the rope a firm yank, making sure the pipe was sturdy enough for his needs. Securing the knot tightly, he answered, "One thing you need to know about my wife is she hates messes. Her doctor diagnosed her with OCD, but in my opinion, he got it wrong. I mean, what clean freak gets chickens? Am I right?"

Fear sank deeper into Haley. Her only optimism was cleaning the floors. *I couldn't clean if I was dead.*

"So, what's your diagnosis?" she spitefully asked. "You probably enjoy fucking little girls, don't you?"

Jeremy answered with a calm voice, "I'm so glad you asked. Have you ever heard of Renfield's syndrome?"

"No, what is it?" Haley sniffled.

"How about clinical vampirism?"

Trembles rattled Haley's brain when she heard the word *vampirism*. Screams burst from her lungs when she made eye contact with Jeremy. She watched him shake his head up and down when he realized she understood her fate. Jeremy pulled out a knife from his back pocket and pressed the steel blade under Haley's left breast. He bent down as if to suckle her nipple and, while still making eye contact, he sliced a three-inch mark into her skin. Blood leaked onto Jeremy's tongue as he moaned with pleasure.

Haley felt a burning sensation rip through her skin as the knife entered her flesh. She watched as Jeremy closed his eyes and ran his tongue along the gash, flicking droplets of her warm, red plasma into his mouth. *This is my time*, Haley thought. She used her arms to pull herself up as she took her legs and wrapped them around Jeremy's neck. She squeezed with every ounce of strength she had and heard the knife hit the floor. Jeremy looked at the knife that fell, and then he smiled as he looked back at Haley. He lifted his other hand, which still held the remote, and with one push of the button,

Haley released Jeremy from her grip. She continued to dance like a marionette until Jeremy finally let go of the button.

The shock from the jolt flung Jeremy flat onto his back, which sent the remote skidding under the washing machine. Without much effort, he quickly rose to his feet and wiped the blood off his face. He cupped his blood drenched fingers together and forcefully rammed them into Haley's vagina, then down into her throat. He smiled a sinister toothy grin and said, "Tastes good, doesn't it?"

Haley was numb to his monstrosity. All hope of escaping forever faded and flashes from her childhood periodically entered her mind. *I'm going to die in this basement*, she thought. *They are not going to let me go when they are finished with me, not like my stepdad did.*

Haley noticed Jeremy was coming down from the high he was on. His hands trembled as he reached for the knife, which still lay on the floor. She recognized his actions were a lot like that of a drug addict, and she knew he wasn't going to stop until his needs were fulfilled. Her mind silenced when the point of the blade entered her stomach. The pain increased intensely as Jeremy gave the handle a slow twist to the right. Horrific screams bellowed from Haley, and Jeremy pulled the knife out and stabbed her again, almost in the exact spot. Haley felt the knife go deep into her at least three more times before she stopped counting. Her words were muffled by the blood that gurgled in her throat as she tried to speak. She looked down and saw Jeremy sucking the blood from the hole which he had created by the multiple stab wounds. Her surroundings were fading, and Haley knew she was dying. A low, piercing keow sound caught her attention, and she used the remainder of her energy to force her head to look behind her. She blinked a few times as she focused in on a familiar seagull that sat outside the basement window, staring at her from above. It flapped its wings and made a few more calls, to which Haley was sure she understood the meaning. *It's time to go home.*

A warm sensation overtook Jeremy as he fell back onto the floor. His heightened elation made him oblivious to the demise of his dangling subject. Blood reached far beyond the towels he had put down, and chunks of meat hung from Haley's lifeless body. Jeremy sighed with gratification, knowing she exceeded his expectations. He rose to his feet as he was ready to hand her over to his wife. Haley's cold, blank eyes stared at Jeremy as he looked in her direction, and he gave her body a hard push to see if she was still alive. "Shit!" he said aloud. He began looking around at the mess he had made and realized he had forgotten to take pictures, so he picked up his tripod and brought it closer to Haley's body to snap a couple of shots when he heard his wife come down the steps. Jeremy closed his eyes, knowing he had fucked up again.

"Tsk, tsk! You promised I could have her this time, babe," Shelby said disappointedly, as she looked at Haley's gutted insides hanging out.

Jeremy raised his inner eyebrows to imitate the expression of a sad puppy dog and playfully tossed a portion of Haley's tissue at his wife's feet. She reached over and picked up the fleshy mass off the floor, then walked over to her husband and shoved it down the front of his pants. "You want to play, do you?" she asked mischievously, while stroking his genitals. Jeremy smiled in light of his wife's erogenous demeanor and decided to take advantage of the situation. He grabbed a handful of Haley's blood and smeared it over Shelby's face. She laughed and did the same to him. They joyfully tossed around more blood, then began making wild, passionate love on the cold cement floor next to Haley's hanging corpse.

Jeremy buttoned up his jeans and watched his wife slip her dress back on when they had finished. Sadness overcame him when he realized his wife did not get to enjoy Haley's services. "Maybe we'll have better luck next week with that new girl that's been hanging out by the gas station," he said optimistically. The thought of her wearing those sheer shorts with the purple G-string, while holding her sign that reads, "Anything helps. God bless," made him so hard.

But that was for another time.

Song of the Summer

by Dylan Wells

Three days down, three to go in the hot, unrelenting sun, unblemished blue sky, and the turquoise waters of the Caribbean. It was a scene out of a travel ad, but Sara was miserable. She was not this person, not someone with sun-kissed skin laughing as the wind threatened to steal her hat, or who walked on a white sand beach with her cover-up billowing behind her. She liked air conditioning and books, and if she had to be outside, she preferred pine to palm. But when a friend has access to a yacht that had more bedrooms than her apartment (a studio, so not hard, but still), who was she to say no? Nevertheless, this wasn't the rejuvenating getaway she'd convinced herself it'd be.

Allie, the friend with the yacht, plucked her earbuds out, then waved to get Sara's attention. Once she had it, she pointed to her ear, signaling Sara to take off her headphones. Sara did, grimacing at the sweat-soaked squishing sound the ear cushions made. Hopefully, a little break in the sun would dry them out. She dropped them on a side table and turned to see what her friend wanted.

"Wanna go back to Nassau? You at least smiled there." The way Allie's skin gleamed in the sun, she could have been a bronze statue of a sunbathing woman, albeit one dressed in a yellow bikini, a giant sun hat, and sunglasses. Didn't Sara's grandmother have something like that? A ceramic goose on her porch she dressed for the seasons?

"I see a smile," Allie sang. "So, is that a 'yes'?"

Even Sara had to admit Nassau was interesting. Under the wear on the colonial buildings, the distant deep drone of a sea shanty and bite of rum hung on the breeze. It was also comfortingly solid land and not the unknown, seemingly endless depth of the sea. Anything could be down there. Long forgotten nightmares. Ancient and angry drowned gods. A never-ending nothingness that got darker and darker until it risked consuming her soul. Sharks. But tourists filled Nassau to the brim this time of year, which was also not Sara's idea of fun, and Allie joked there hadn't been any attacks from forgotten nightmares in years.

"No, just thinking of something dumb." Sara collapsed next to Allie.

The vinyl was only a few degrees shy of blistering the backs of her death-pale legs. She forced herself to take a deep breath and keep her exhale long and slow. Lying motionless, with the breeze, the gentle rocking of the boat, the lap of the waves, a haunting melody that carried over the waves from somewhere, some of the tension drifted from her body. Maybe this wasn't so bad.

"I'm sorry. I know I'm being a drag," she said.

"I'm used to it."

Sara peeked to make sure Allie was joking before telling her "fuck off" with a laugh.

A sudden, loud thump interrupted the waves, accompanied by an impact that canted the boat slightly and set it adrift.

"Did we hit something?" Sara asked.

"Don't be dramatic. We're in the middle of the sea—what's there to hit?" Allie leapt up and stalked to the railing.

That meant *something* hit *them*. Sara's mind ran through possibilities, flashing from "I am the captain now" pirates to undead cannibal pirates in an instant. No, she told herself. Allie was right about her being dramatic. It was probably nothing.

"Oh, shit," Allie said under her breath, then louder, "Sara!"

"What is it?" Sara ran to the edge, beating Allie's response by a breath just as hers refused to leave her lungs. There was a tangle of debris, a net, fiberglass pieces of boat, and–

"A body," Allie said.

Adrenaline pushed more sweat out of Sara's overworked pores. The body was recognizable as male, salt crusted, covered in meaty sores and blisters, lips white from the sea and dehydration. He wasn't bloated or waterlogged, more like a mummy. A husk.

Allie said she'd get help before dashing away. Sara shaded her eyes to peer toward each horizon for any hint of where he'd come from, but only water blending with sky surrounded them.

The corpse's hand twitched.

Sara froze, except for the strands of her hair caught in the breeze. He wasn't breathing. But his hand moved again, jerky as if reanimating into something she hadn't considered—zombie pirates!

A scream built in her throat when the hand lifted again, testing its reanimation. Then a crab skittered out from underneath and slid into the water with a plunk.

"For fuck's sake," she whispered, almost laughing at herself, but hysterics crowded the gates and would flood through any opening.

The body lurched up, sunken eyes wide, mouth open and distorted, hair a seaweed-like tangle.

She managed to scream this time. The zombie pirate's gaze turned to her.

"Please." The man's croak barely made it to her.

He was alive.

They got him aboard with difficulty. His skin was so loose his hand risked degloving when Sara pulled his arm over her shoulder so her stronger legs could drag him out of the water. Allie hoisted herself back on deck after him. As the braver and stronger swimmer, she leapt in to guide him around.

"The water feels weird." Allie made a face as she rubbed her thumb and fingers together.

"Gross," Sara said, glad she hadn't jumped in.

"So beautiful," the man murmured.

"Not now, buddy." Allie gave Sara a "can you believe this guy?" look.

Together, they dragged him to the galley, though they had to find their way to deposit him on the table in darkness because the light wouldn't turn on. His scrawny legs, bare from just above his thigh down, dangled over the edge. Sea-thinned blood trickled out of the newly opened sores and dripped onto the floor.

"Don't worry." Sara dribbled water into his mouth between his moans. "Help is coming."

"About that," Allie glanced at the barely conscious, barely-a-man and back to Sara before deciding to speak. "No one answered. I couldn't even get a radio station. We're not that far from land, but there was no one."

"Then we'll head towards the help."

"We can't. Nothing worked. Not the radar, not the motor, not the electricity, not even the SOS. We're stuck here."

"And what could have caused that?"

"Nothing! It's not possible. I double checked everything before we left. Everything was fine. The SOS has its own power source, but it's dead."

"Flare?"

"Only works if there's someone around to see it." Allie raised her shoulders along with her eyebrows.

"Well, fuck." The surrealness of the situation staved off panic, but didn't offer any solutions.

Wait. Wait just a damn minute. Sara walked back into the scorching sun, scouring the horizon again. There had to be another boat out here and close. The music she heard earlier was loud enough that she could make out words, though she couldn't understand them.

"There's nothing," Allie said.

"There's music. Listen."

Allie tilted her head to listen just as it swelled.

"See! That has to be a boat! Where is it?"

"Uh-oh." Allie slapped a hand to her forehead, then told Sara she'd be right back.

"What 'uh-oh'? It's beautiful. I need to get their playlist." Sara stepped to the railing, letting the song wash over her as Allie retreated. Maybe it would be easier if she were in the water. More deliberate, like getting out to walk. Yes, that was it. She'd just jump in. Why had she been so unnerved by the water before? It called to her now and when she gazed into it, an impossibly beautiful woman with huge eyes tread water below. The woman reached her slender arms up and Sara reached back. Their fingertips brushed and—

Allie's Pilates-strong arm pulled Sara back so they both toppled to the deck. The woman followed, rising from the water like Botticelli's *Birth of Venus*, minus the shell. Glossy tendrils of her hair stuck to her skin, and Sara needed to...

"Shut the fuck up!" Allie's screech sliced through Sara's mind like a scalpel just in time to witness Allie punch the woman in the throat. The woman's song cut off with a gag and it wasn't a woman at all, but something with teeth longer than Sara's fingers and crammed together under dark, vacant eyes. Viscous film coated its rot gray skin and trailed where it touched, including the deck. Thanks to it, Sara's attempts to scramble away were terrifyingly ineffective. The tinny beat of a pop song blared from the earbuds in Allie's ears, and she fought in time with the beat. Then the creature's fishtail swiped Allie's legs from under her, so she slipped under the railing and into the sea.

"No!" Sara screamed. The creature's song returned, faltering and hoarse. It morphed briefly into the woman again, but it was a lipless mouth that brushed Sara's grimacing one. Sara tried to push it away, but it was too slippery. Sara whimpered just as the creature latched, humming a dirge that calmed the fight in Sara's limbs. The tension left her body. It was perfection.

A rhythmic pounding joined the hum. Foot falls at a run. Then Allie, still soaking wet, slid across the slime, slammed into the creature feet first, and sent it careening over the side.

Headphones blaring a song Sara hated snapped over her ears. Then Allie helped her to her feet. They couldn't hear each other, so they didn't speak, but didn't have to. Sara exuded "what the fuck" like the creature emitted mucus, and Allie's apologetic grimace told her she'd tell her later.

For hours they sat in the galley in the dark with the dying man, serenaded by pop music until the lights turned on. Only then did Allie remove her earbuds and speak.

"Sorry, that hasn't happened in *ages*."

WHEN YOU DON'T BELIEVE

BY MEL KITCHING

"*He sees you when you're sleeping, he knows when you're awake,*" I sang along with the rest of the school choir during my seventh grade Christmas concert. Both of my parents were in attendance; I spotted them out in the sea of faces, sitting next to my younger sister, Lucy.

"Well done, kids! Families, thank you for coming as always. That's a wrap on the 2024 Winter concert!" Miss Rynone, our choir teacher, cheerfully beamed into the microphone. Upon her cue, we exited stage left, eager to find our families and go home. Christmas was in six days; and there was so much left to do. Our small northeastern town always made a big deal of it; there were lights on every house, every street; even lampposts were carefully decorated with shiny, multicolored Christmas bulbs. Our town hosted a plethora of Christmas events, and you couldn't walk more than three feet down any street without hearing holiday tunes blaring from every

direction. Needless to say, Christmas was a big deal around he
re.

I found my family, and we left the school together, stopping
at the closest Dunkin' Donuts on the way home for hot
chocolate. We decided to drive around and look at the lights
and decorations; a tradition we had had since I was four: hot
chocolate and sightseeing. The next day would be the biggest
day of the holiday season in my town. We called it "Santa's
Social," a gathering where the whole village got together and
decorated the large pine tree in the middle of the shopping
center; complete with hot chocolate and cookies being handed
out at tables, stations for crafts and games such as a sled race,
the tallest snowman competition, cookie decorating and so
much more. Lucy's favorite was the station where kids get to
sit down with Santa himself, telling him what they wished for
and whether to expect them on the naughty or nice list.

I wasn't feeling the holiday spirit this year. Seventh grade
had sucked so far, and I knew of a few other kids in my class
that felt the same way. Middle school was a drag, and the magic
just wasn't there. I blamed it on getting older, but even the
adults participated and acted like Christmas was the best thing
since TikTok was invented, so I knew there was something
deeper going on.

"Cheer up, buttercup," my mom said happily from the
front passenger seat. We had driven down almost every road
in our town, seeing inflatable Christmas lawn decorations,
houses with so many lights that it made me wonder what
their electric bill looked like, and my personal favorite—the
house with an inflatable setup of The Grinch battling Buddy
the Elf with blowup swords. We were making our way back
home, finally. "Gavin, what's the matter? You *love* Christmas!"
She turned on the car's Bluetooth speaker and blasted holiday

songs, clapping and singing along. My dad and sister joined in, but I found myself resting my head in my hand and staring out the car window, wishing they would just shut up.

"Hey, bud. It's only a few more days. You know what happens if you don't participate. Just suck it up, buddy, and have fun with us. It'll be over soon." My dad reached around his seat and patted my knee. *You know what happens if you don't participate.* Mom and dad would donate all my gifts to charity if I wasn't in the Christmas spirit, but for some reason, I still couldn't find it in me to care.

Later that evening, we had gone home and settled in for the night, turning on some cheesy Hallmark movie where a small-town baker falls in love with Santa Claus himself. The movie was so boring; I found myself dozing off on the couch halfway through. Lucy had been asleep since the first fifteen minutes of the film; she was a lot younger than me and couldn't stay awake much past nine o'clock. I woke up as the end credits rolled. I rubbed my eyes with the back of my hands, ready to head to my bedroom, when I heard my parents talking in hushed voices in the next room. I stood up slowly and made my way to the wall, pressing my ear to it to snoop on my parents' conversation.

I heard a few words here and there, but I couldn't make out the full story. They had mentioned Nate Baxter, and that was enough to send chills down my spine.

Nate disappeared last year, and his case was still cold. It was right around Christmas time when he was reported missing. His parents were found murdered in their living room, and as curious as I was, my dad wouldn't tell me any of the gory details.

A sinking feeling formed in the pit of my belly, so I decided to cut their conversation short by entering the kitchen, rubbing my eyes and yawning, pretending I had just woken up.

"Hey guys, I'm gonna head to bed now." I walked up to my mom and hugged her, and my dad used his hand to ruffle up my hair. I noticed them exchange worried glances; something in their eyes said *he didn't hear any of that, did he?*

"Goodnight, kiddo. Make sure you get some rest for the event tomorrow." My mom kissed my forehead, and it was then that I noticed the empty bottle of wine on the counter in front of her.

The next day, we got up bright and early to get ready for the big day. The list was as follows: snowball fight, snowman contest, cookie decorating and hot cocoa, sled race, and then my parent's favorite: pictures with Santa.

I was getting too old to sit on Santa's lap, but for some reason, my parents still forced me to do so. I didn't feel bad about it because all the other kids in my grade still did. In fact, there were some older kids from my school that got photos with Santa, too. I braced myself for the day ahead. I did enjoy the snowball fight and sledding, sure, but what pre-teen boy wouldn't?

We arrived at the village center. Families were already there, signing in, their faces full of glee and anxiety about today's festivities.

I don't remember much from the festival, other than winning the snowball fight (it was like a game of dodgeball, if you're hit, you're out). I won a first-place medal and a cool little snow globe, which Lucy decided belonged to her, but I didn't care much, anyway. I shook it for her, and she was instantly mesmerized. It showed Santa in the middle, reindeer on either side, and it rained glittery crystal snowflakes when you shook it up.

The other thing I remembered was sitting with Santa. As my parents got their photo op, I got to tell Santa what I wanted, which, naturally, was a new gaming console. I knew it was just a man in a suit, and that my parents would be the ones buying the game system, but I obliged to make my parents happy. My mind switched back to their conversation last night, and my face went slack.

"What's the matter, little boy? Not afraid of Mr. Claus, are you?" Santa uttered a low voice into my ear and my parents snapped their photos, beaming at me and occasionally sending a thumbs up my way.

"No, sir." I replied in my best confident voice. The vibe that Santa was giving off was an eerie one; his tone of voice sending shivers down my spine. I tried to stand up, ready to get the hell out of there, but something stopped me; physically holding me down. Santa's arm wrapped around my waist, holding me tighter, not allowing me to leave.

"Good. Because I can *smell* fear." He growled in my ear; a low, guttural voice exuding from his thin, cracked lips. "Tell me, Gavin, how do you think I travel so far in just one night, huh? I'll give you a hint: it's not caffeine. It's *certainly* not milk and cookies. No, this stuff is better. This stuff is premium. And I get it from little girls and boys...like...*you.*"

I swear I'd never jumped up so fast. I broke his grip around my body and ran back towards my parents; my heart beating out of my chest and my palms sweating profusely. Chills ran down my spine, goosebumps prickled my skin, and if I had been looking in a mirror, I guarantee my face would have been white as a ghoul.

"Mom! Mom," I shouted, making sure my parents could hear me and weren't going to leave me alone with whatever that *thing* in the Santa suit was. "Mom," I said as I finally reached her, "that's not Santa." I finally stopped running, pausing to catch my breath as I rested my hands on my knees. I panted like my old dog Barkley, who had crossed the rainbow bridge two years prior.

My mom laughed. "Of course that's Santa sweetie! Who else would it be?" She looked over at my dad, and I realized how much I hated that simple little gesture. One adult glance, one knowing exchange between two adults that somehow kids just couldn't quite seem to understand. I wanted to be in the know. I was desperate to know, just once, what they were thinking.

"You don't understand, mom, he said something weird. He scared me..." I looked down at my feet, ashamed and feeling slightly embarrassed to admit that Santa Claus scared me. I stole a glance back over at the big man in the red suit, hoping not to make eye contact, when I realized Lucy wasn't with us: she was next in line to sit on Santa's lap. The man saw me stealing glances in his direction and sent a menacing wink back towards me, lifting the young boy from his lap and reaching his hands out for my little sister next. "No!" I cried.

I sprinted over to the chair, no longer caring that I was causing a scene. I ripped through the ropes holding people in their spots in line, ignoring the pleas and cries of the many parents who were more concerned with me skipping the line than they were with the alarming man who was disturbingly close to their children. I could feel the sweat beading on my forehead, and the fact that I was dressed in my best snow clothing didn't help. If anything, the heavy, clunky outfit weighed me down and made it harder to run towards my baby sister.

"Lucy, get away from him! We're leaving, now!" I shouted, finally reaching her and grabbing her arm with my gloved hand. Her eyes were twice their normal size; she was every bit scared as she was confused, and I could tell she was slightly disappointed, too. This was her favorite part; she had been waiting all day for this moment, and here I was, ripping it away from her...but I didn't care. I needed to get her away from that ma n.

"I am so sorry, folks. I don't know what's gotten into our boy," I could hear my dad apologizing to the townsfolk, walking down the line, offering shaky smiles and assuring everyone I was fine. I didn't want to make a scene with my parents, so I bolted for the parking lot with Lucy in tow. She was now crying; wordless, sniffly sobs, occasionally using her glove to wipe her nose.

As soon as we reached the car, my parents caught up, forcing us all to climb in. "What the hell was that!?" my dad shouted, and it sounded more like a demand than a question.

"Dad, you don't understand! He said something to me. He said—" I had started to stammer, but my dad cut me off abruptly.

"I don't want to hear it. I've had enough. Straight to bed when we get home. Oh, and no cell phone for the rest of the day."

I laid in my bed that night, replaying all the events of the day. When I had finally fallen asleep, I had a horrible dream about Santa. In my dream, I was sitting on Santa's lap, giggling and sharing sugar cookies, when all of a sudden, he grew two more arms with enormous claws, making their way towards me. I looked back at Santa, expecting him to be laughing as if this was all some silly prank, but what I saw instead petrified me. Santa's eyes had turned completely black, his pupils lost to the sea of darkness, and his teeth were razor sharp, like something out of Jaws. He laughed maniacally at me, and his mouth grew; stretching like a snake about to swallow a rabbit whole.

His teeth were positioned right over the top of my head, and his four arms held me tightly in my position. I wriggled and writhed, kicking my feet into his shins, but he didn't let up. His mouth started closing, closing, closing...down on my head...

The next few days at school were utter torture. Every kid in the school had either heard about or witnessed my outburst, so naturally, nobody wanted to talk to me. I sat alone at lunch, waiting for someone to join me, but knowing it was wishful thinking. I mainly kept my head down for those next few days, pretending I was invisible.

Christmas Eve arrived. I tried my best for my family to keep my spirits high, but it was nearly impossible after everything that transpired. We went caroling with a few other families that evening. I did sing along, but my heart wasn't in it, and it showed. By the time we got back home, it was late, and we had all decided to head to bed. The rest of my family was anxiously waiting for Christmas morning to arrive; eager to get to sleep just so that they could wake back up and open gifts, but I was just ready for it to be over.

I awoke around one o'clock in the morning on Christmas Day. I heard scuffling in the living room, and I lay frozen in my twin bed. Lucy and I had tried to catch Santa in the act before, successfully failing each and every time. I remembered being younger and tiptoeing across the hall to her bedroom, shaking her awake and pressing my fingers to my lips to signify that we needed to stay quiet. Together we would waltz out to the living room, as silent as can be, but we had always just missed him. There was one time that we swore we had caught him.

Lucy insisted she saw something shimmying up the fireplace, but I wasn't so sure. I knew he had been there, though, because there were fresh cookie crumbs littering the counter, and the glass of milk had a small drop of liquid slowly falling down the side of the cup as if someone had just sipped from it.

I was shaken from the happy memory by more sounds emitting from the living room; I could hear low grunts and what sounded like paper being ripped apart. My thoughts raced. What *do I do?* Something didn't sound right. Every fiber in my body told me to stay in my bed where it was safe, but curiosity got the best of me. I slipped out of bed in my red plaid pajamas, throwing on my wool slippers as I headed towards my bedroom door. I could hear my heartbeat in my eardrums as I reached for the doorknob; my hands were shaky and sweaty as I made contact with the cold, brassy object.

My eyes squeezed shut as I turned the knob slowly, trying not to make a sound. I opened the door just a sliver; enough to take a peek with one eye through the crack. I could hear more clearly with the door opened, so I pressed my ear up to the open sliver in the doorway, straining to listen more carefully.

I heard Santa's *"Ho, ho, ho!"* except it wasn't normal. It sounded evil, guttural; a maniacal sound coming from deep within his large gut. I tried to peek out into the room, but all I could see was the hallway, so I slowly and cautiously opened the door a little more. I snaked my way out into the hallway, trying my best to tiptoe, and peered around the wall with my back pressed to it.

What I saw by the Christmas tree shattered my heart into a million little microscopic pieces, like a Christmas tree ornament hitting the ground.

Every gift had been torn open; the wrapping paper strewn all over our carpeted floor. I saw the box to a brand-new gaming system, but the system itself was smashed up and dented, laying on its side. I saw headless dolls littering the room, with their limbs pulled off and naked. A pink dollhouse for Lucy lay upside down on the floor, and it looked like someone had taken a baseball bat to it. A new pair of sneakers for me were sitting in the fireplace, flames swallowing them whole. And then I spotted the culprit: the big, white-haired man in the red suit sat, leaning against the wall next to the tree with his legs sprawled apart across the floor, clutching his stomach as he laughed. I pressed my hand to my mouth, fighting back tears.

I wasn't mad about *my* gifts. Hell, I didn't even care about the stupid holiday anymore. I was pissed, for Lucy's sake. I was already losing the Christmas spirit, but Lucy? She was fully immersed. This would forever change the way she saw the holidays.

As I kept looking around, taking in my surroundings, I noticed the walls had been painted red; streaks running down and making a *plopping* sound as the droplets hit the floor. *Lucy's new art set*, I thought, remembering she had asked for one of those kits full of paints and markers that dried out after one use and cheap colored pencils.

I took a step back. My intentions were to back away into my bedroom slowly, without Santa noticing that I had ever been there. I realized my mistake once it was already too late: when I stepped backward; I hit a hanging picture frame with my head, sending it barreling down to the floor. Santa's head snapped in my direction. My body turned to ice; frozen in place, I couldn't feel my hands or feet.

"Where ya' going, little boy? Is someone afraid of ole' Saint Nick?" the jolly old lunatic asked. He rose to his feet, causing more tears to flow from my eyes. My fight-or-flight mode kicked in, sending my feet racing up the stairs to my parents' bedroom.

"You're not going to like what you find up there! I left something *extra* special; a little gift. You know, since I destroyed all the other ones!" The white-haired man laughed as he slowly ascended the steps after me. He was making it no point to hurry as he clutched his belly in one hand and held the railing with his other.

I started shouting for my parents; warning them of my arrival, trying to get them to wake up before I even reached the top of the steps. As I arrived at their bedroom, my hand clutching the brass doorknob, Santa had caught up to me. He leaned forward and whispered, "*This is what happens to little boys who don't believe.*"

I turned the knob and all the blood drained from my face. My dad lay on the king-sized bed, bound to the bedposts with Christmas lights around his wrists and ankles. His eyes had been gouged out, and in their place were two bright, sparkly red Christmas tree bulbs. The pillow beneath his head was soaked with red liquid; gore still seeping from the wounds where his eyes once were. As I looked around, taking in the scene, I realized he had been stabbed repeatedly in the abdomen; his entrails were fully visible, and the only thing holding them in was a ginormous golden ribbon tied tightly around his waist.

I bent over and vomited, not caring that I was spewing bile onto the carpeted floor. Snot bubbled in my nose and the tears wouldn't stop flowing as I threw up all of Christmas Eve dinner and the heap of neatly decorated sugar cookies I had snuck before bed.

As I got back to my feet, I noticed my mother hanging from the ceiling fan in a similar fashion to my dad with the

Christmas lights. I wish I could say that the hanging was all she had endured, but the reality was much, much worse. She has been stripped naked and her breasts had been cut off; large green bows tied from ribbon replacing them. I noticed something sticking out from the top of her head, and it took me a minute to put the puzzle pieces together. Her hands had been removed and were fashioned on top of her head to look like reindeer antlers. Droplets of blood were oozing down the severed hands, dripping onto her face, which was in a permanent state of horror and fear. Blood smeared the walls all around the room, and it was then that I realized the red substance on the walls downstairs was not at all from Lucy's art set.

"LUCY!" I shouted, realizing that I was the only one who could save her now. I pushed past Santa, and surprisingly, he let me. I barreled down the stairs, my stomach tightening again. I didn't have time to stop and heave, though. I needed to get to my sister. A disheartening thought crossed my mind as I neared the bottom of the stairs: *what if she's already gone?*

I reached her bedroom and slowly opened the door, afraid of what I might find. At first glance, the room appeared empty. She wasn't in her bed, and I nearly had a heart attack thinking of all the things that sick bastard in the fuzzy red suit had done to her. I kept searching, waiting for the gruesome scene to jump out at me, when I noticed her squatting in the corner of the room with her head tucked into her lap. She was shaking vigorously, and although I could tell she was trying her best not to cry, I heard suppressed little sniffles coming from her direction. I ran over to her to make sure she was okay.

"Lucy! Oh, my God, are you okay? Did he hurt you?" I asked, examining her up and down. She didn't seem to have a scratch on her body, from what I could tell. She whispered something that I couldn't quite understand through the sobs. "Huh, Luce?" I asked.

"I saw mom and dad," she whispered again, her cries getting louder. I pressed my hand to her mouth before hugging her, simultaneously telling her to quiet down and that I understood.

"I did, too. We have to get out of here. Come on!" I stood up, my little sister clutching tightly to my arm. My back was to the door, but I could sense something approaching the doorway.

"I tried to warn you... but you didn't listen. Now it's time for me to fuel up!" The man said, following up his sentence with that sadistic laugh of his. "*Ho ho ho!*"

"*Gavin!* Look out!" Lucy cried as I felt a stabbing sensation in my neck. Red hot pain seared through my body as I felt what I could only describe as several knives piercing my flesh. I was still semi-conscious at that point, but I didn't have much left in me. Dazed and confused, I watched Lucy throw a lamp at Santa, sending him stumbling backwards away from me. I pressed my hand to the wound in my neck, wincing as I touched the area. Pulling my hand away, I glanced down at it, covered in blood. I felt hot breath on the back of my neck, and I heard a distant scream. I could tell it was Lucy, but it sounded like she was a million miles away. I spun around just in time to catch a glimpse of the cause for my wound: Santa sported razor-sharp teeth, my blood dripping from his mouth as he smiled down at me. I became lightheaded and felt my body starting to fall to the floor, but the demonic man had caught me before I hit the ground. The last thing I felt was the blood draining from my body as he took another bite into my flesh.

Three years later

"Lucy?" the nurse knocked on my door, carrying in a tray of food with her. I inspected the plate, making sure it was exactly how I liked it.

"Thank you," I said, removing the noise cancelling headphones from my ears. I carefully lifted them off, making sure it was safe to do so before fully committing to the act.

The nurse sat down on my bed, watching me eat my food carefully. She cleared her throat and placed her hands in her lap. "I have some news for you," she said, eyeing me cautiously. I put down my fork and swallowed the bite I had been chewing.

"Hmm?" I asked, afraid of where this was going.

"You're going to be getting a roommate. I know, I know, trust me. But we're overcrowded right now. We need the bed, Lucy." I sighed in annoyance, continuing to shovel food in my mouth.

"Fine. As long as she knows my requests." *My requests.* No Christmas music, no decorations around my room, no ham, because that was what my family ate every Christmas Eve. No holiday spirit.

The last roommate I had ended up with a broken jaw and scars across her face. She taunted me, singing *"Deck The Halls"* while prancing around the room. My instincts had taken over. I became animalistic, scratching and clawing at her mouth with my nails, leaving her bloody and clutching her face. I pinned her to the ground and decked her repeatedly in the mouth while screaming at her to *just shut up!*

I was placed in solitary confinement for a month; and once I was released, it was under special circumstances: no roommates; I got to wear headphones around the holidays, and I got to pick my own special meal for Christmas Eve dinner. The age range of the girls in the institute was eight to fourteen, and since we were all still fairly young, the nurses liked to decorate our rooms with ornaments and lights and our own table-top mini Christmas trees. My room was skipped, of course, per my request.

That night, my new roommate, Andrea, showed up. We got along pretty well for the most part, and she mainly asked me questions about the institute. *Is the food any good? Are there any cute male nurses? Do you have any friends here?*

We had gotten settled into bed, and I couldn't help but feel a little sorry for Andrea. The poor girl was spending her first Christmas in a mental institution, and I wouldn't allow her to feel any sort of holiday spirit. She told me she was admitted because she sees things that other people didn't see. I'm assuming they stuck her with me because they had also diagnosed me with schizophrenia, even though I haven't seen a thing that isn't really there. I tried to tell the doctors, the therapists, the nurses...

I said goodnight to Andrea and rolled over to face the wall. I wondered silently how long she would be here; how long we would have to share a room. Maybe this one *would* work out, maybe we'd become friends. I liked her so far, and she seemed to be right around my age, about eleven or so.

"Goodnight," she replied, tucking herself into her sheets. "Lucy? Can I ask you something?" She asked softly, and I rolled around to face her.

"Do you have any family that visits you for Christmas?" My soul left my body the second she said the words. I froze up in terror, shock overtaking my body.

"I don't have any family. And didn't Nurse Picco tell you? You can't talk about Christmas with me." I said sharply. So much for being friends.

"I know, I'm sorry. I just wanted to ask. I'm sorry about your family. Do you want to tell me what happened to them?" She asked, placing her hands under her head.

"I can tell you, but you won't believe me."

"Sure I will!" She said reassuringly. "I'll tell you a secret if you tell me. Okay, here it goes. So, I see things. I've been diagnosed with schizophrenia. We know this, but one time, I pushed a boy off the top of the playground on purpose. I told everyone that I didn't realize it was a person. I thought I was seeing a monster. But I knew it was him. I caught him taking pictures up my skirt on the monkey bars. So I did it... I pushed him. And I used my diagnosis as a crutch."

Her confession had made me relax a little bit. I took a deep breath, ready to divulge my version of events to her. "Okay, fine," I said, taking a deep breath. "It was Santa. He killed my family."

Andrea laughed before saying, "you're kidding, right? Santa isn't real."

"STOP! Don't say that!" I screamed, running over to her, throwing my hand over her mouth. "You can't say that! He'll come for you!" I screamed. She started yelling for help, clawing at my arms, trying to remove them from her mouth. Nurse Picco rushed in, followed by two other nurses. *Here comes solitary confinement,* I thought.

For some reason, Andrea took the blame for what happened. She told them that she set me off by asking about my family and Christmas time; that she didn't mean to upset me, and that she wasn't worried about sending me to solitary. I was, however, forced to take a small dose of olanzapine, and was placed under watch until it kicked in. I was getting tired anyway, and soon, I found myself falling deeply into sleep.

In my dream, Santa broke into the institution, leaving a round, plaid-wrapped gift, tied neatly with a bow at the foot of my bed. When he left my room, I climbed out of the covers, eager to see what he had gifted me. I carefully unwrapped the object, my heart racing as I peeled back the gift wrap. My heart sank into my stomach when I saw a pair of eyes staring back at me. The gift Santa had left me was my brother's head.

I awoke in a cold sweat, realizing the nurse was gone and I must have been long passed out. I looked to the foot of my bed and sighed in relief when I didn't see a decapitated Gavin sitting there, wrapped in plaid. I stood up to head towards the shared bathroom, when something caught my attention. Andrea wasn't in her bed.

"Andrea?" I whispered, wondering if she had woken up and headed for the restroom as well. I started to feel bad, thinking that maybe I had woken her up from my nightmare; maybe I had been shouting in my sleep. I stepped out into the hall, void of any life since everyone else was sleeping silently, and I reached the bathroom.

As soon as I clicked on the bathroom light, I screamed. Andrea's lifeless body was propped up in the corner of the room against the wall, blood pooling down around her and snaking its way to the drain in the center of the floor. Her wrists had been slashed and covered up with gift tags; her mouth had been sewn shut with holiday red ribbon. A bright silver bow sat atop her head, and above her, on the wall, read "From Santa" in bright red blood.

A crowd gathered around me, all rubbing their eyes as they had just woken up and exited their rooms upon hearing my screams.

I spent the rest of my time at the institution in solitary confinement. Nobody believed me when I told them I had found her that way. The rumors flew around the building. *Andrea pissed her off by bringing up Christmas. She's a psycho. Everyone knew she would snap one day; of course it would be on Christmas Eve.*

"Lucy, can you please explain to me why you would do such a thing?" my therapist asked. I continued to look down at my feet, avoiding his gaze. I had told him the story several times at this point, and I was at my wit's end. So this time, instead of reciting the story, word for word, I stood up and headed for the door. Two guards waited for me on the other side of the door, straight jacket in hand, ready for me to exit.

I took a deep breath in as I prepared my new answer:

"Because that's what you get when you don't believe."

A Murder of Crows

by Ali Toothman

Cadence brushes her sleek black hair, ensuring perfect symmetry all around. Scissors snip at her bangs, ensuring the correct length. A bit of blush adorns her face, followed by careful swipes of mascara on her already long lashes, and lipstick to complete her look. She has to look her best or Patrick will have a fit when he gets home, despite her imposed captivity.

She walks out of her attached bathroom and into her carpeted bedroom to finish getting ready for the day. Cadence makes her bed and heads to her closet to choose her outfit for the day. Once dressed, Cadence prepares for her favorite part of the morning.

She grabs two trays with twine handles from under her bed. One is filled with trinkets, buttons, crystals, and other shiny bits and baubles. The second remains empty. Carefully, she begins her descent.

She trudges down the wooden staircase with care to ensure she drops nothing. With both arms holding the trays, she can't hold the railing. The thought runs through her mind, *What if I just take a tumble? Will this all be over?*

When she reaches the lower floor of her home, Cadence sits the two trays onto the table and separates them. She takes the empty one with her to the stocked pantry and places a bag of circus peanuts and sunflower seeds into it. Next, she goes to the refrigerator, choosing the strawberries and grapes. Cadence walks across the kitchen to the counter to cut up the fruit.

She lays out a spread of fruit, nuts, and seeds within the tray, then picks up the other and heads outside. The trays sit side by side as she arranges the trinkets in one and the food in the other, ensuring the trinkets are in an even layer across the bottom.

Her yard is a perfect rectangle surrounded by a wooden privacy fence, which makes it the perfect place to enjoy her mornings with her friends. She lays both trays on the grass, a few feet away from each other, before retreating into the house.

Cadence trots up the stairs and into her library, then reaches for her own wooden lidded box on the bottom shelf of her favorite bookcase. Within it holds her tarot cards and a bag of crystals. She grabs both, returning to the backyard, a smile lighting up her face.

While Patrick, her husband, is at work for the day, she can do the two things she loves most: read her tarot cards and spend time with her crow friends. Patrick isn't fond of birds or "witchcraft," as he calls it. The last time he caught her with oracle cards, he threw them in the fireplace and accused her of summoning demons in *his* house.

Cadence holds her cards in her hands, clearing her mind of the awful thoughts running amuck and focusing on her intentions. She splits her deck in two in front of her and thinks, *What is my card of the day? What message do you have for me?*

Then she slips the cards through her hands and pulls the card on top: The Wheel of Fortune.

A smile graces her lips—what good fortune this card can bring. She grabs her guide book, opening to The Major Arcana section to search for the Wheel of Fortune meaning. Alongside the picture of her card, the description says Wheel of Fortune brings karma, good luck, ends destructive cycles in life, new opportunities, and tells her destiny is in her hands.

Her smile brightens with this message as she stares at the page. She grabs her daily journal and writes down her card, the meaning, and her interpretation and feelings about it.

I'm thrilled with this card! Things have been tough lately with Patrick. As things get worse at work, the worse he gets at home.

I feel as though I put good karma out into the universe, so hopefully, some comes back to me.

I'm excited about the change of luck! Maybe that means things will get better here.

It's been pretty tough for me here lately and I just need a break. I need some good things to come my way and I'm ready for it!

As she finishes writing her notes, she notices her crow friends joined her. Some pick through the trinket tray while others grab peanuts and other snacks. They squawk and flutter their black wings with excitement. Her smile remains as she returns her attention to her tarot cards.

"I clear the energy of these cards. Bring good karma and happiness my way. Thank you for your help today," she whispers to her cards before kissing them and returning the cards to their bag.

Cadence moves her hands over her crystals, waiting for a *feeling* about which one she needs to carry for the day. She waves her hand over the red and orange carnelian, clear quartz, the speckled lepidolite, the perfectly purple amethyst, and settles on green aventurine. Her bright white teeth flash as her smile reaches her eyes. She remembers green aventurine is for good luck and believes it goes perfectly with her card for the day. Cadence tucks the green, sparkling crystal into her pocket and puts the rest of them away in their silk bag, then returns them to the table.

The crows continue picking at their pretties and snacks for the next hour before they flutter away. Cadence walks to the trays that lay in the green grass and lowers herself to inspect the trinket box. Her day brightens once more when she notices the crows have left her gifts today. Every now and again they do, and it makes her day every time. Along with her tarot cards and crystals, she keeps the gifts from her crows in the box in her library.

She carries the trays back into the house and heads towards the trash can under the sink. Cadence throws away the remaining fruits, then puts the peanuts and sunflower seeds into plastic bags. She writes the date on them and takes them to the pantry to put in the bin with the bird seeds for her feeders.

She goes back up the stairs to tuck the crow's trays under her bed; for safe keeping and to hide them from Patrick's prying eyes. There are some things she needs to keep to herself, and this is one of them. Cadence loves her morning routine with the crows and doesn't intend to let him ruin it.

An odd, angry thought pops into her head. *Patrick only hates what he doesn't understand.* She shakes her head, trying to clear the message. She didn't enjoy having these kinds of thoughts because they only ever lead to hurt and a potential fight, which always ends in tears and a black eye. Thinking about the way he is brings more heartache.

After ten years, Cadence still hasn't gained the gumption, nor money, to walk away from Patrick. He won't let her work and rarely allows her to leave the house, which is why she loves her time with the crows. Despite being birds, they're her only friends.

Things used to be wonderful between Cadence and Patrick. Once they got married, he started to get angry over the littlest things. Two years into their marriage, the abuse turned physical, and it only got worse from there. By then, he had alienated her from her friends and what little family she had left.

Her sisters no longer spoke to her after Patrick blew up at them and accused them of trying to take Cadence away from him. Out of fear of Patrick, she said nothing to stand up for them. At that moment, she lost her remaining family, because her parents had died when she was a teenager.

Cadence continues her therapeutic breathing exercise to bring herself back into the moment. She decides now is a good time to do yoga and work on grounding herself. She changes into workout clothes, swaps the green aventurine into the pocket of her new pants, and heads to the backyard.

She rolls out her yoga mat and begins stretching. Cadence looks around at the trees and sees the crows watching her from afar. Lifting her hand to give a slight wave, she notices the man next door is outside on his back deck. She gives him a wave instead to keep from odd looks at her waving to trees. He walks over to their gate and gives it a knock.

"How's it going? It's a beautiful day today," he says as Cadence undoes the latch and opens the gate.

Cadence gives him a shy smile and agrees. She wrings her hands in front of her and avoids eye contact. *If Patrick knew I was talking to him, he would make sure I face the consequences.*

They make small talk for a few more minutes before Cadence excuses herself. She rolls up her yoga mat, goes back inside, and locks the door behind her, silently hoping Patrick doesn't find out.

She remembers the last time Patrick found out she had talked to another male and she shudders. He had broken her arm that time. She can only imagine what would happen if it happened a second.

With her plans foiled, Cadence decides she's better off reading.

Cadence goes back to her study and grabs *Misery* by Stephen King from her shelf. She moves to sit in her favorite chair, an overstuffed papasan complete with her favorite throw blanket. She sits down and leans over to turn on her wax warmer. Despite being summer, fall scents always bring her joy.

A few hours and over one hundred pages later, Cadence hears the one sound she hates more than anything—Patrick's car pulling into the garage.

She jumps up, tossing the blanket back into the chair, and turns off her wax warmer before running down the stairs to meet him. When he walks in, she's standing with her hands folded in front of her with a smile on her face.

"What the fuck are you smiling about, huh? That you're fucking our neighbor?" Horror flashes across her face as quickly as his fist hits her cheek.

Cadence stumbles backward, hitting her back against the wall and knocking a picture frame to the floor.

"Oh look! Now you're breaking our wedding pictures! I bet that's exactly what you want, isn't it? A divorce so you can go fuck the neighbor guy? Huh?" Patrick steps forward and swings his fist again, but Cadence moves in time, infuriating him even more.

Before he can hit her again, Cadence runs out the back door and into the middle of the yard. It's usually a safe place because Patrick won't hit her except behind closed doors. He barges out, slamming the door behind him. Taking a swift glance around, he finds no signs of prying eyes. He snatches Cadence by the hair, slaps her across the face, and drags her back into the house as she begs him not to hurt her.

Patrick may not have seen anyone, but he did not escape observation. Hidden in the shadows, someone heard Candace's screams and plotted to do something about it.

The next day, Patrick stays home from work. Despite her begging and pleading, telling him he's wrong, Patrick still believes Cadence is cheating on him.

When he arrived at home the day before, their neighbor was outside working in his yard. He waved to Patrick before he got the garage door open and walked over to talk to him. The man asked how he and the wife were doing and mentioned seeing her this morning and chatting with her. While remaining calm in the face of his neighbor, his blood boiled, and he took it out on Cadence with swift action.

Patrick gets up at his usual time, five a.m., and wakes up Cadence along with him and demands she make him breakfast. While he eats his meal, he notices black birds landing in his yard and goes ballistic.

He storms out the back door and grabs a handful of landscaping rocks and throws them at the birds, yelling at them to get the fuck out of his yard. Cadence begs him not to and that they aren't harming anything as he shoves her aside and to the ground. He stomps toward the birds as they take off and throws another rock, hitting a crow mid-flight.

Patrick storms back into the house, giving Cadence an "Eat Shit and Die" look as he passes her. Cadence sits in the grass of their backyard and silently pleads to the gods that no one heard them nor will try to step in. When someone tries to save her, it gets that much worse.

As the day goes on, Cadence hides in her study reading *Misery* while Patrick watches sports highlights. She tries to drown out the sound of him yelling at the television by listening to Lo-Fi music in her ear buds. With her music playing, she didn't hear Patrick yelling for her. She found him standing in the doorway to her room.

He enters her study with a beet-red face full of anger and hatred. She yanks out her ear buds and asks him if he needs something. He stalks over to her and stands above her, demanding she make him lunch. Before she can agree, she raises her hands to protect her face on instinct. He laughs at her fear and walks away.

After lunch, Cadence heads back to her study, her safe place, as Patrick yells to her he's going to do yardwork and clean up the mess "those fucking birds made" with the rocks. She rolls her eyes and continues toward her destination.

She puts her ear buds back in and starts reading.

Without realizing it, hours have gone by. She's finished her book, and Patrick hasn't been in to demand dinner.

She goes looking through the house and calling for him, but all that greets her is silence. Cadence hopes he's fallen asleep in front of the television and has opted to leave her alone. She makes her way to the front yard to see if he's out there, goes to the garage and he isn't there either. The last place to look is the backyard.

She opens the back door and a scream rips through her body and the neighborhood.

Crows surround Patrick in the grass in the middle of the backyard, pecking at him. She runs over to Patrick, ignoring the birds as they shuffle out of her way and some fly off.

The first thing she notices is Patrick's eyes are gone. All that remains is gouges and rivulets of blood streaked down his face. His face bears the marks of being torn to bits, with cuts and gashes covering him. When she checks his pulse, his head falls to the side and his mouth opens, showing that his tongue is missing. He has gashes along his neck and injuries to his ears.

While Cadence was reading her book, her crow friends decided to take care of her problem for her.

When Patrick made his way to the backyard, the crows kept a close eye on him. They watched his every movement and waited for their time to strike.

The crows made their way into the backyard while his back was turned. When he turned to face them, before he had a chance to yell, the crows attacked him, ripping at his throat with their vicious beaks. Removing his Adam's apple had made it impossible for him to scream for help.

Patrick fell to the ground, grabbed at his throat, despite the horrendous pain, and tried to hold pressure to stop the bleeding. He flailed back and forth as the crows pecked and ripped at his body. They tore at his arms as he tried to shield his face. The moment he moved his arms, the birds dive-bombed his eyeballs, ripping them from his skull.

With the agonizing pain of their attack, Patrick was rendered helpless with the inability to scream for help. He tried to stand to run away, but tripped and fell to the ground. He tried to hide his remaining eye while holding his throat. The crows took the opportunity to peck at his ears, rip out his hair, and rip at any exposed skin. When he removed his hand from his remaining eye, it ripped from his skull with a swiftness he would have never expected.

He realized his fight was futile, and the end was near. He continued to bleed out of every orifice the crows had ripped into his body.

By the time Cadence had found him, it was far too late to save him.

Cadence called the police in hysterics, begging them to send an ambulance. It didn't take long for the medics to place Patrick on a gurney and cover him with a white sheet and await the coroner's arrival.

Cadence looked up at the trees and saw her bird friends. Though terrified, she sent up a silent thank you to them.

Months went by and Cadence had been working at her new job, the life insurance money had come in, and she was getting into a routine of her own.

It didn't take long for her to get Patrick's belongings packed away or donated. Though they had been together for so long, she found she didn't miss him at all. The pain, anguish, and beatings were over. She could talk to whomever she wanted, have friends, get a job, and not worry about much of anything anymore.

While her crows pecked away at their snack box and searched for pretties, she went through her tarot journal and stumbled upon an entry from a few months prior. A small smile broke out across her lips as she put everything together.

She had put good karma into the universe, and the universe had given it back to her.

Through the Silvered Looking Glass

by Jules Terry

The train came to a screeching halt; the gears grinding against each other as if in terrified protest. Mia was propelled forward by the sudden halt. Her temple hit the opposite wall hard, and her eyes were momentarily blinded with stars and blackness at the edges. When she stood, she made momentary eye contact with a custodian clutching a side rail. He averted his eyes and quickly turned in the other direction as soon as the locomotive was immobile.

"What the f—" Mia muttered before being cut off by the screeching sound system.

"The train is experiencing engine trouble. Your current tickets will be honored when the train is running again. Parts from Hamburg should be here in three to four days," she heard the message repeated in English. Then, once again, in a handful of other languages.

By the time she had made her way back to the compartment filled with her travelling party, the custodians were ushering people off the train.

"But where are we?"

"Will we be refunded for lodging?"

"I am missing a meeting with a partner! This is bullsh—" She tuned out the noise. Her head was throbbing from the impact it had received, and she had to focus on where the hell in Luxembourg they were.

Mia chose to stay behind at the B&B when Sheila and Brock went out to explore. They claimed it was a food expedition. Gary had stayed behind and was blessedly silent for once. He quietly watched the news while she rested her eyes. Perhaps making it the one time the two had been amicable with one another.

While the newscaster droned on in German, Mia drifted. She found herself in blackness when she opened her eyes. She knew she had hit her head hard, but hadn't thought it was enough to take her into the night.

Her body felt weightless—the way it is when coming out of unconsciousness but could easily slip back into a doze. Her hands came to her face to rub the sleep from her eyes. She still felt the sensation of fatigue before she was ushered into reality, heart pounding into her sternum like the door Brock threw into the wall.

"We just found out how to kill the time in this dump! Some crazy hoot was raving about the castle not far from here." Brock threw to-go containers of food on the small table in the room and unceremoniously dug into the modest meal. Sheila carried on the tale, snacking on the hard cheese and pork sausage they had scrounged up.

"He was prattling on in Luxembourgish, and I can't say we got all the details, but it sounded fascinating. The castle has been abandoned for years, according to legend, and was originally the home to some magician or mad scientist," Sheila paused, gauging the others' reactions. Brock sat stupidly, his mouth overstuffed with bread and cheese. Gary was enthralled. The fog from sleep still hung around Mia, making it hard to focus. Sheila frowned at the apparent lack of enthusiasm.

"*Well...*" Sheila drew out the word, dripping with condescension, "apparently, there is supposed to be this ballroom with a floor made of silver-backed mirrors, with all these mirrors on the walls. He kept saying something about the full moon, which just so happens to be tomorrow. Brock and I were thinking we could make it a day trip and get some pictures of the room during the full moon."

She paused; her smile plastered on with a retort ready for anyone who disagreed.

Without surprise, Brock's shadow agreed without hesitation. Mia's brow furrowed as a trace of her dreams attempted to claw to the surface of her consciousness. The pounding in her chest had stopped and her heart dropped like lead to her stomach.

Say no. The thought ricocheted before being silenced by the glowering and hopeful faces staring at her. Her smile didn't reach her eyes when she nodded her agreement.

The rest of the afternoon was spent tracking down any information they could on the stone monolith. The locals were reluctant to speak with them or share information. Many would bless the Mother, the Father, and the Holy Spirit. Most would walk away. Fate smiled at them when they came to the bakery. The old woman, unnervingly grim and blind in one eye, gave them a discontinued map of the town. It held landmarks they couldn't find on the tourist map from the train station, one of them being the castle.

Mia glanced back at the old woman as they left the shop and received a toothless grin. The old woman pointed up at the ceiling and waggled an arthritic finger in goodbye. The opaque, blind eye seemed to stare into another realm beyond the group of friends.

An involuntary shudder ran through Mia as she caught up with the group, who had already determined the castle was a couple of miles away. It would take a couple of hours to get to it if they allowed sightseeing along the way. Gary had resumed his constant chattering, completing the chipmunk-like façade he wore.

Mia looked at Sheila's glassy-eyed expression and knew she was tired of the mansplaining.

"Guys, let's leave first thing tomorrow, bring the necessary snacks and what-not, so we can be back by the afternoon." She saw Gary gearing up to object and quickly added, "They mentioned parts could be in by the third day. We don't want to miss catching the train to Düsseldorf by camping out and not making it back in time."

The weight in her gut lifted a touch as the others nodded their agreement. Gary wouldn't argue if it meant getting out of this hovel sooner.

Brock clapped his hands. "Well, that's settled. Let's get some more grub, a pint, and pass out."

A disquieting silence greeted Mia and the group the following morning. The hustle and bustle they had seen from the previous day was absent. Mia soon realized the town was deserted as they made their way toward the trail on the map. The chickens, goats, cats, dogs, and people were nowhere to be seen despite the sun rising fast in the east.

"I can't wait to meet a fairy or an elven prince at the castle! Who knows what kind of fairytale creatures come out when the full moon is out," Sheila cooed.

"Yeah, Frau Holle is going to give you spiders, wolves, or a witch who will dump tar and feathers on you. There will be no gold left to a castle left to looters and squatters," Gary heckled.

It grew silent afterward while Sheila pouted. Gary had a bounce in his step for getting under her skin. Soon, they were silent due to the overgrown path, which hadn't been tended in years. They had to backtrack a couple of times when they came up against foliage too dense to push through.

Mia fell and skinned her knees at one point when a branch snagged at her shirt, refusing to release her.

Brock disturbed a beehive, and it fell from the tree it was in and burst into a writhing mass of black and yellow revenge. Sheila ran screaming through webs and past dark crevices, screaming the word *EpiPen* over and over.

When they were finally released from the grips of the forest, which was reluctant to let them go beyond its fortifications, they were met by the gothic-style behemoth. Overgrowth ceased, the forest giving space to the stone giant. The trees appeared to bow back in awe, like the small group of hikers did now .

Or, perhaps, Mia thought, *they are trying to get away from it.*

There were spires and turrets they could see rising above the grey stone walls. The black iron gate was drawn open, the pointed spikes of the bars hung down beneath the edge of the stone gateway. The forest had been protecting them from a frigid breeze they could now feel gusting along the path, urging the small group forward. They were through the gate and made their way to the wooden doors. They opened without so much as a squeal from the rusted hinges.

Much to Sheila's delight, and to Gary's dismay, the entry hall was surprisingly clean of the grime and cobwebs they had expected. In fact, for a structure no longer printed on tourist maps, it was well taken care of. The marbled floors still shone. The velvet curtains and the furniture were free from dust or the destruction and decay time gave rise to. It took them little time to find the ballroom, which stole their breath once they were through the open door.

The room was a sweeping circle. The vertical mirrors were posted every few feet along a seamless stone wall. They were larger than anticipated. Above, the ceiling opened to what had once been a circular, stained-glass work of art. Now, only the bones of the iron framework and broken colored glass remained. In the center of the stone floor was a large, circular mirror below the opening in the ceiling.

Mia's body screamed at her to flee in the opposite direction, yet her feet carried her toward the object in the center of the room. Mia looked into the glass. "Holy shit, guys, you have to see this!"

Shocked gasps echoed around the room. One pack *thwacked* to the ground as the others approached the mirror. There was a slight curve to it, convex, as if half of a lens was installed into the ground. They could see the planets aligning, as if through a telescope. The full moon was at the very center—a cratered pupil staring up, waiting.

Light filtered into the room, refracting from the mirror. It cast shades of neon purple and green and red toward the dozens of mirrors circling the room. Slowly, the glowing orb in the middle, which had appeared to be the moon's reflection, moved toward the group, settling at their feet.

It stared into them.

The room fell into chaos.

Sheila screamed. She turned and ran for a door no longer there. She stumbled from mirror to mirror, sobbing with each failed attempt to find the door. "Where did it go?" she screamed. Brock and Gary joined her, trying to use flashlights and metal water bottles to shatter the glowing glass without success.

"What the fuck is *happening*?" Brock choked out, his voice hitching on the last word with a sob.

Mia continued to stare into the eye, hypnotized by the celestial alignment she was witnessing in the mirror.

As the planets completed their calibration, the pupil moved back toward the center. The room burst into a hazy light, filled with glowing dust motes. The frames around the mirrors glowed brightly, forcing each of them to squint and shield their eyes for a few moments.

It was Gary's turn to scream.

The collision caused by Sheila's fleeing was a jarring shock back into reality. Mia finally looked around the room.

Creatures were pouring from the mirrors, which had become portals with the alignment. There were monsters who had tentacles falling from their chins. Some looked like aliens from children's drawings or old conspiracy photos of Area 51. The worst of them were like the demons who might crawl from the depths of hell—their blistering and horned skin red or black, eyes opaque and glowing unnaturally.

The horror of the situation finally registered with Mia. This wasn't her dream. She was here. These creatures of other worlds were coming in through the doors made of silvered glass.

One of the monsters grabbed Brock, who had stood stupefied by what he saw. Brock punched the praying mantis-like creature to free himself. His fists flew, his feet kicked out. Mia blinked, and Brock's head was gone.

The creature screeched in triumph and launched the lifeless body toward the two women. The corpse sailed over their heads and through the glass. They watched as the body floated off towards the rings of a planet resembling Saturn.

The women looked at each other. What Sheila saw on Mia's face finally broke her. She began screaming. Her eyes were bloodshot and bulged from her face. What was left of Gary, who thought he could use a silver tongue to get his way, was being dragged toward them. Toward the portal.

"We must go, Sheila. *Now* or *never*," Mia pleaded with her remaining friend.

The answer she received was a terrified screech, and Sheila pushed herself away from Mia. A lizard-like being, a cross between a dinosaur and a comic book villain, turned its attention to the women. Mia shakily pushed herself back to the edge of the looking glass. Her breath caught in her throat as her fingers passed through the mirror.

Her friend's scream echoed in the chamber as she was dragged into the sea of creatures. Mia barked a laugh as she realized they looked similar to young adults at a disco or a rave. *Come to planet Earth, party, and get a taste of the locals.* Sheila's screaming had stopped abruptly.

Mia looked over her shoulder. The pupil was once again staring at her. For a moment, she caught a glimpse of her own reflection in one of the pocked craters. Her eyes had taken on a haze similar to the baker woman's.

With a calmness she couldn't have imagined possible before this night, Mia crossed her arms over her chest. She fell back into the unknown and its embrace, content to exist in weightless suspension until she was called.

KILLER QUEEN

BY CHRIS HEINICKE

Tonight is the night. Silas muses as he enters Shapers nightclub at eleven p.m. sharp on a Friday night. Bodies pack close together on the dance floor, and he spots multiple targets ripe for the taking.

But he needs only one.

He looks over the selection. With his good looks and suave demeanor, luring a victim will come easy.

Silas cuts a sharp figure in his leg-hugging black leather pants, white button-up shirt, knee-length buckle-up boots, and pitch-black trench coat. Although the light inside the club is dim, he sports a pair of dark sunglasses. He pauses, seeks out the main bar, and heads in that direction.

His thirst must be quenched.

A couple of barflies who occupy the area as though they pay rent allow him the smallest amount of room possible to wiggle through and order a drink. He opens his mouth to speak.

"Excuse me, please," a sweet feminine tone stops the words before they leave his throat. "Might I be so forward as to suggest a cocktail to a complete stranger?"

The words from her lips, fastidious and precise, and her piercing emerald eyes hold Silas's full attention. Dressed in a sleeveless, long, lacy black evening gown, her raven hair in a single braid drapes over her shoulder and points downward as if inviting him to look. Her pointed red stilettos put her at a height just a few inches short of him, even though he stands at six feet four. Thumping dance music, idle chatter from those seated at the bar, and the clinking of drinks fade into insignificance. He smiles as the woman removes the sunglasses that cover his eyes and holds an open palm in front of him.

He nods, encouraging her brazenness. "Please do."

She smirks and clicks her fingers a few times to draw the attention of the middle-aged, balding bartender. The man smiles at Silas's new drinking companion, but Silas knows a fake smile when he spots one. "A Gunpowder Gelatin for the sharp dressed man and a Moët et Chandon."

The bartender nods and goes about getting the two newcomers a drink. "Silas MacNair," he offers a hand to the lady.

"Adeline Shaunakshi." Her dainty, well-manicured fingers touch his hand.

"A lovely name indeed." He raises her slender fingers to his mouth and tastes them with a gentle kiss. Floral scents rise from her pores to his nostrils, proving to be congenially intoxicating. "You smell delicious."

Adeline whips her hand away from him. "Let's not get too presumptuous." She turns to the bartender. "Mr. MacNair is paying."

Of course he is. Silas keeps a slight smile plastered on his face, and hands a twenty-dollar bill to the barkeep, who appears as though he won't release his grasp on the two drinks until he sees cash.

"Keep the change," Silas swaps the money for the drinks, bringing the Martini glass and champagne flute toward him. Normally a single malt scotch fan, drinking from anything but a whiskey tumbler, is foreign to him.

Adeline thanks him as he passes the Moët to her. "Here's to new acquaintances, and a night of memories to come." Silas holds his glass high for her to clink hers to it.

"I bet."

They each take a long sip of their drinks. The fruity flavors dance on his tongue while the bubbles tickle his nostrils. Although delicious, he can't see himself consuming a second 'Gunpowder Bang Bang,' or whatever it's called.

Exchanging small talk while sipping their beverages, Silas notices a pair of cute dimples form each time he elicits a giggle from her. Small talk soon graduates into a conversation where they learn more about each other. Silas soon discerns Adeline's heritage stems from an Estonian baron, technically making her a baroness, which she admits doesn't comfortably fit her.

"Another drink, my lady?" he asks.

"I shall decline, in favor of a dance, my lord." She grins, those dimples reappearing.

"It would be remiss of me to neglect a lady her desires." He grasps her hand with his and allows her to lead him to a place on the dancefloor. Taking a quick glance at the bar as they depart, he catches the bartender staring at him while speaking into a telephone. As much as he wants to walk over to him and ask him what the fuck he's looking at, he deems Adeline a more favorable use of his time.

Although not a fan of the 'doof-doof' music blasting throughout the venue, the dance will serve in his favor as a prelude to a ritual he hungrily desires to share with her. Among the packed throng of people pressing their bodies against each other as the bass thumps throughout the club, they squeeze their way between many people of all sexes, all of them smiling as Silas unintentionally brushes against several women's scantily clad bodies. Feeling overdressed, he guesses he and Adeline must stand out like a pair of sore thumbs. But if Adeline is concerned, she doesn't let on. Turning her back to him, she grinds her lithe body into his, the friction causing a severe stirring within him.

"Oh yes, I'm feeling delighted too," she purrs.

They dance for what feels like hours, but as Adeline excuses herself to go to the bathroom, he flicks his wrist to look at his watch and discovers only a couple of hours have passed since he entered the club. The night is still young, and full of possibilities. Keeping an eye out for Adeline, he retreats to the bar and gets a whiskey neat. The barman from earlier is nowhere to be seen. A younger, far more pleasant barmaid serves him, and although he wishes to confront the bald bartender, the chance to pour some Glenlivet down his throat is an opportunity he relishes.

The hair on the back of his neck stands on end as he feels a light finger tap on his shoulder. Casually turning, his smile beams as Adeline stands before him. Was there ever any doubt she would return?

She whispers into his ear, "Come back to my place."

He accepts her offered hand, keeping his enthusiasm under wraps as his hunger spikes.

Fucking. Awesome.

Having ascended the stairs, they now stand at street level. The illumination of the full moon high above shines brightly, and a cool breeze blows. Silas notes the sparkle in Adeline's eyes as she looks temporarily fixated by the celestial body.

"It's beautiful," he whispers. "Like you."

She blinks a couple of times and turns back to him. "Thank you."

While other people scurry from one place to another, he and Adeline dawdle arm in arm. The wind picks up a little, a chilled bite to it that immediately causes one's bare skin to shiver. She snuggles in close to him; her face seeking shelter from the elements inside his unfastened coat. He's only too happy to oblige her need for comfort.

"I've never seen you at Shapers before, but as soon as I saw you walk in, I knew you were the one." Her soft tone ignites his interest.

"If I'm honest, Adeline, I actually followed a pair of young blondes wearing belts as skirts."

She giggles. A row of cabs parked parallel to the sidewalk wait ready with drivers behind the wheel of each. As per tradition, those seeking passage select the front-most vehicle. Silas opens the back door for Adeline, who enters and slides along the seat, allowing Silas to make his entry. Adeline leans forward and whispers into the driver's ear. He nods and turns the music louder.

"So, do you think we can make it back to my place with our clothes still on?" Adeline smirks at her suitor.

"I will try my best," Silas answers, just before Adeline slides along the seat his way, the hem of her dress riding up her thighs as she does so. Their bodies touch, and he cups her cheek and chin in his hand. "But my lady, you are so irresistible."

They move their faces closer, their lips touch and soon, after a breathless minute, their tongues dance together. Each of them moaning, hands wandering over each other's body, the cab comes to a stop.

Panting, Adeline disengages from the kiss, and points to the vehicle's window near Silas's head. "We're...here..."

Silas finds himself in the unfamiliar position of feeling light-headed. "Okay," he whimpers, energy momentarily sapped from his usually virile being. He's used to having the upper hand. He fumbles for the door-release lever and pulls it up while pushing the door open fully.

His vigor returns almost instantly. He stands next to the cab and extends a hand for Adeline to grasp and pull herself out and up on her feet. Not knowing where they are now, he relies on her to guide him.

"Hey, that will be twenty bucks," the cab driver yells through the window.

"He's paying," Adeline smirks.

If Silas could even consider being irritated with her, she flashed those disarming dimples again. "Of course I am. Sorry, my good man," he walks over to the driver and completes the transaction by placing a fifty-dollar bill in the man's hand while shaking hands with him.

"Oh, wow. Thanks, my man. You need a lift home after your little rendezvous here, just call me at 555-1124."

Adeline raises her eyebrows and shakes her head, appearing disgusted by the cab driver's lack of decorum. She reaches for

Silas's hand upon his return from paying the cab driver, and points to the building ahead of them.

Impressive, he nods upon seeing the illuminated foyer of the apartment complex with its high ceiling, marble counters and suited doorman standing by, ready to greet them and approve their entry. "Good evening, Miss Shaunakshi." He nods at Adeline and glances curiously at Silas. "Good evening, sir."

Silas nods back, his gaze on the back of Adeline's neck, the palm of his hand warm from her touch. The glass doors slide open automatically for them, and Adeline greets the bespectacled middle-aged lady seated behind the counter as they pass her to head for the elevators.

Adeline presses the 'up-arrow' button, and an audible ding sounds as the elevator doors open for them. Snuggled together, the receptionist flashes them a knowing smile as they step in and turn around before the doors hide the sticky-beak from their sight. "We have thirty levels to ascend, and then you can take me, handsome."

Their bodies close in on each other again and engage in another passionate kiss, Silas gently pressing her against the wall. She jumps, wrapping her legs around his hips, rubbing herself against him. He finds his breathing intensifying again, his skin beginning to sweat. Running his hands up her thighs, they reach her smooth, bare ass. "Oh, you're a naughty little minx," he whispers in her ear.

The grin she gives him is sly, reminding him of a cat. "You have no idea, my lord."

Another ding, and the elevator doors open to reveal a pair of grand wooden doors, framed with black metal edges and matching hardware. "Is there a castle inside?" he asks, gently lowering Adeline down to the floor.

"Not quite, but it's fit for a queen," she almost purrs as she walks up and pushes one door open.

"Wait, there's no lock?"

The dimple-creating grin returns to Adeline's face. "I own the whole building."

Silas's eyes light up. How rich is this woman? He follows her inside, his jaw almost dropping upon spotting the cavernous entrance room, its size larger than an entire inner-city apartment. On the far side of the room, windows extend from the floor to ceiling. Silas guesses the height to be around thirteen feet. Several chandeliers hang from the ceiling. The carpet is a white shagpile of some type. The furnishings are of little consequence to him.

Adeline caresses Silas's arms. "Go make yourself a drink while I freshen up. And then..." she dances her fingertips over the curve of her hips. "Get ready for me to rip you apart." She bites her bottom lip and looks him up and down as she walks away. He watches her throat as she walks from sight, disappearing through another heavy wooden door to a room unseen, and he smiles.

She's going to be mine; all mine.

Built against the opposite wall, he sees a small bar area. Several bottles of Moët et Chandon fill up two shelves of a refrigerator, decorated to look like a Victorian lady's pretty cabinet. On the wall adjacent to the cabinet is a large painting of a regally dressed woman who looks like she could be a long-gone ancestor of Adeline's. Her face, Silas could swear, is identical to the woman 'freshening up' for him.

On another shelf he finds what he's seeking, a bottle of 24-year-old Glenfiddich single malt. He locates a whiskey tumbler and fills it halfway, then swallows half of it in a single gulp. *Nice.* He nods and makes his way to a black leather couch, situated a few feet from one of the towering windows, and looks out over the city.

Perhaps he has met a worthy prey at last. What could be better?

"Oh Silasss…" Adeline says in a singsong, purring voice. "I've got something for you…"

He turns his head and sees her leaning against the doorframe of the room she used to 'freshen up.' The bedroom? Her long, black hair is no longer fastened in a long braid. Instead, it flows freely, as one arm holds it in place over her breasts while her other hand placed between her legs, shielding that piece of heaven from Silas's hungry eyes.

"Oh yes, Adeline." He stands, unable to do more than follow her lead now.

As he walks, she winks at him and turns around, giving him a complete view of her beautiful, round ass. Starting with his jacket, he slowly disrobes on the way to her, taking his time so that he'll be wearing nothing but a pair of white cotton boxer shorts once he reaches her. Entering through the doorway, he finds himself in an even grander room, lit only by the full moon through a giant floor to ceiling window. A four-poster bed presents itself as the obvious location for their upcoming lovemaking, but a set of shelves against the wall opposite the window halts him mid-step.

"What. The. Fuck?" he asks out loud.

Three long shelves, packed full of mason jars, each reflecting the moonlight from outside.

A trick of the light, surely.

Silas shakes his head, losing sight of Adeline as he walks up and takes a closer look.

All but one jar contains a severed head.

Frederick Mustaphson 1776.

Deacon Maybrian 1798.

The labels seem to taunt him with their casual delivery of names and dates.

"Adeline, what the fuck is this?" He strides toward her to find her pressed face first against the window, arms outstretched.

She moans, and he freezes. Her skin darkens from her natural porcelain. Her head trembles, her hair falling out, and her ears shrink from sight as a new pointed pair sprout on top of her head. Short dark hairs pop out all over her body, and a tail extends from her tailbone.

He lets out a sharp gasp. "You're a—"

Adeline turns around, cutting him off as he stares. Her face has changed, her round emerald eyes are now slanted, and fine whiskers sprout from either side of her feline nose.

"Meow." She fakes a purr and throws her head back, giggling. "I take it you've seen your jar?"

He doesn't respond to her straight away.

She knows nothing of who she's dealing with.

"Are you going to kill me now?"

Adeline flicks her hands. Her fingers point at the ground, long blade-like claws extend from the tip of each one. Her eyes light up, and a sly smile grows almost ear to ear. "You catch on pretty quick, Silas." She tilts her head slightly to the side as he approaches. "You're not going to try to run? Or plead for your life?"

He shakes his head. "No. It's me who's doing the killing, my lady."

She tilts her head back and laughs. "Oh, you're so funny. I think I like you, but it's full moon, and I need to feed. Just offer me your throat, and I'll make it quick."

"You offer me yours, and I'll promise you the same."

Adeline wrinkles her feline nose. "What makes you think you can take me? I could cut you down in a second."

Silas nods and veers a couple of feet away from her to approach the glass. Not only can he see the colorful lights of the city and the bustling activity on the streets below, but a faint reflection of Adeline's still perfect feminine form. She might be more cat than human, but no less delectable. "Notice something?"

She stops dead in her tracks, raises her clawed hands, and hisses. Silas chuckles.

"Why didn't you tell me?" She points to a nonexistent reflection in the window. "I could have broken the truce between our clans."

He turns and faces her. "You think I would have just stood here and let you kill me?"

"I can surely take you, but not all of your kind, vampire."

"So now what? I could strip these little shorts off, and we could just fuck." The truce didn't apply to him; he didn't belong to a clan. At least that's how he saw it. He could fuck her and then take her throat.

Adeline purrs, rubbing her face with her wrist. "I need to feed before sunrise. My hunger increases." She closes her eyes, allowing her body to transform back into her human form. Silas watches the transformation, expressionless. "Get dressed and help me catch some prey."

He contemplates killing her now, but with his suave nature he can easily lure a young woman, or man, for both of them to feed on. Maybe after that, some crazy fucking. "Okay, let's go then. I'm hungry too. Woman or man, I'm not fussy."

Adeline locates some matching underwear and puts it on. "Wait, I get the feeling you don't care about the truce." She frowns at him.

A thudding crash nearby draws their attention.

The pair of them spin and face the doorway to the room. Silas leaps forward, rushing to investigate the source of the sound, but a swinging fist appears as if from nowhere, giving him no time to duck or dodge. Striking him in the nose, his vision blurs immediately and he falls to the floor on his back.

"What the hell was that?" Adeline asks, still only partly dressed.

Silas groans and picks himself up off the floor. "Come out, whoever the fuck you are," he snarls. Upon seeing the lithe figure of a woman appear a couple of feet from him in the doorway, the whites of his eyes turn red and a pair of fangs extend from his canine teeth. "Did you order takeout?" he asks Adeline.

"Oh my, she does look tasty," Adeline says. "All wrapped up in black leather, too." She points at the newcomer. "Why did you come here?"

Without saying a word, the petite woman vanishes from their view. Silas and Adeline exit the bedroom and run into the large, open living area. A loud bang fills the room as the power immediately cuts out, filling the room with darkness. "Where'd she go?" Silas asks. Despite his ability to see in the dark, he can't see her.

What the fuck now?

Leaning her head back and pushing her chest out, Adeline harnesses the power of the full moon, her body shaking during the few seconds needed to make the change to full werecat.

Silas bares his fangs, desperately seeking the intruder. *How can she be masking her scent?*

A rapid double chink sounds out. Adeline groans and slumps to the floor, blood pouring freely from her chest.

Silas stares in shock as the fluid he most desires spreads on the floor. Forcing away the impulse to gorge on the blood, he moves to her, keeping an eye out for the perpetrator. Two shiny metal spikes stick out from her body. "Adeline?" he asks, bending down to take a closer look at her injuries.

"Fucking bitch... silver," Adeline coughs up a spray of blood, her eyes glazing over as her life force rapidly drains from her being.

Shaking with the need her warm blood inspires, Silas groans, and releases his hold on the dead shifter. "Come out, bitch, and fight me properly," he calls to the slayer.

The sound of heavy boots hits the floor, and he turns quickly, catching sight of the predator holding a crossbow in one hand, and a long wooden stake in the other. He dodges a bullet sized wooden spike, missing him by less than an inch and embedding itself into the leather couch.

"Who the fuck are you?" he asks the impossibly nimble woman. Although not the first time he's fought a slayer, this one seems quicker, almost as though she can predict his movements.

Maybe she isn't human.

She ducks into the shadows again. Silas panics, fear flowing through his veins for the first time in over a hundred years. "It's been too long since I've encountered a worthy opponent."

He turns his head from side to side with every step he takes, circling the couch area and setting forth to the bar. "Why don't we talk about this?"

"I don't negotiate with killers," the woman spits in an emotionless tone.

He spins around, his movements guided by his inhuman reflexes, but the woman has already dispatched a wooden stake from her hand, slicing his wrist open as the point travels all the way through. Growling at his enemy, pain travels all the way to his heart like an electrical current. The split second spent reeling from the injury gives the woman enough time to throw another stake, and he finds his other wrist the target of her attack.

"Fucking bitch," he spits at her. Claws extend from each of his fingers, and he launches himself in the air, slicing at her with both hands.

The woman's thick leather jacket absorbs the razor-sharp fingernails, and she rips a longer wooden stake from her belt and stabs him in the side. Silas crashes into the ground, bleeding profusely from the fresh wound. "No one calls me a fucking bitch, vampire." She stabs him through the stomach using such force and speed, the stake becomes embedded into the wooden floorboards beneath the shagpile carpet.

"How the fuck..." He coughs and sprays blood into the air.

"I stabbed a demon once, after he killed my mother. I've been training to kill fuckers like you since I was a child, and now, I'll be getting paid big money when I deliver yours and Adeline's heads to the one who put a contract out on both of you." She takes a seat on the couch near the bleeding Silas. "I couldn't believe it when I got the tip-off at the bar that you were both there."

He finally gets a good look at her face. The barmaid. He chuckles, spitting up blood while doing so, as she takes out a long silver blade. "Hold still," she smirks as she brings it to his throat.

As the moonlight catches the silver blade, the name *Bella Morris* engraved catches his eye.

"It will be over before you know it. They don't call me Killer Queen for nothing."

"I... know...you..." he coughs up more blood and feels the pointed knife enter his neck.

"Fuckdammit," he whimpers, his world turning black as his 456-year-old body meets its end.

THE PERSON

BY DENVER WHEELER

I feel the sharp edge of the blade piercing my skin as the knife slices along my wrist. Pain shoots through my arm, and I feel lightheaded, as if I could faint to the ground at any second. Blood wells up around the wound and drips onto the bathroom floor, tinging the cracked grout with a deep maroon. I want to escape, but find myself unable to move, paralyzed by something beyond my comprehension. The person before me wields the knife but does not hold me captive, so why can't I move? Fear clouds my mind like fog settling over a city, and I feel a deep sense of panic and dread. My body grows heavy, as if hands reach up from the tile to pull me down, dragging me into their dark and frozen world.

"Why are you doing this to me?" I whimper.

The person doesn't respond, but chuckles under their breath. Their long hair hangs in front of their face, obscuring their features from view. I can't tell who they are. Their chuckle rumbles through their chest, a sound that could curdle fresh milk. I shudder and look down—I don't want to see them anymore. I feel myself shake and shiver, and wonder if this could be the end for me. The knife's blade gleams in the person's hands as they kneel to the ground in front of me, staring through those sheets of hair. They contemplate where to cut me next and run a pale finger across my collapsed leg. The sensation sends goosebumps across my body, and I need to find a way out of this.

The bathroom, *my bathroom*, is tiny. I've always felt trapped in here when showering or getting ready, and I wonder if my attacker knew that. Took advantage of that. It's the only space in my house without windows, the place where we would shelter from a tornado if we needed to. Too bad there's no way to shelter from this storm. The caressing of my leg doesn't stop and I feel like the walls are closing in on me. I try to remember how this person got into my bathroom, but I can't. There are walls up around my memories, blocking me from getting in and seeing this situation through a clear lens. All I can see is pure blackness in my mind.

"Please." I say, desperate for this to stop—desperate to save my own life. "Please, I have a family."

They pause in their gentle caress of my leg and cock their head to the side, curious. Their hair shifts but doesn't part, doesn't reveal who they are beneath. I think about reaching my uninjured arm to brush the strands aside, but fear holds my muscles in place, like a marionette controlling a puppet on strings. I wonder what they think of my family, if they know them. Could they be doing this to hurt one of them? They cast their head back down and slide the knife across the blood pooling on the floor. Brilliant red smears across the tile floor, spreading it like jelly, and they seem proud of their work. They reach down a finger and draw a circle in the blood, tracing the same route over and over. I watch in silent horror, wondering what will happen next.

They lift their bloody finger up in front of my eyes, forcing me to look at my own blood. My stomach turns queasy as I watch my attacker withdraw their hand and stick it under their sheath of hair. They suck that finger with a loud slurp. I retch, but nothing comes up—my body is growing weak. I hope they won't lick my blood again as I try to calm my mind. I need to think of a way out. My only chance may be to overpower them, as slim as those odds feel. My weak body can't even stand, let alone fight someone for access to the door. Hopelessness swirls in my mind, quickening my breath, as the person jumps back from me, frightened all of a sudden. They hit the door to the bathroom with a loud thud that echoes through my house behind the door. They whip their head around as if startled that the room had an end, as if they thought they could keep goin g.

A small spider crawls next to my limp and bleeding arm, unaware of the blood dripping onto the floor. As it reaches the pool, a leg gets caught in the blood, soaking it up its fur, and the spider collapses to the ground. I watch the spider drowning in my blood, just as I am drowning in fear and confusion. Realization dawns on me—my attacker is afraid of the spider. I reach out with my uninjured arm to grasp the spider, finding nothing can be more frightening than this situation.

No thoughts of spider bites or sticky webs flood my mind as it would have before. All I can see in this tiny spider is a way out, freedom. I can grab this spider and throw it right into that thick curtain of hair. My mind creates a vivid picture of how my attacker would flail and squeal with fear, leaving the space for me to scramble to the door, body willing. Just as my hand reaches the spider, their hand darts out and snatches it up first.

Blood drips down their hand as they hold the spider. I look up with wide eyes and can see their body shaking around that long hair. Their fear is palpable as they hold the spider between their blood-smeared fingers.

"It's alright to be afraid," I try, hoping I can work an escape from this moment, instead.

The person freezes in place. The shaking stops. I've never met someone like this, never experienced such bizarre and dangerous behavior. My mind cannot fathom what they might do next. Quick as a flash, the hand holding the spider darts toward the person's face, parting the hair and popping the spider straight into the flat mouth. I can see the lips on the person—they are thin and cracked, hardly moving as the mouth crunches down on the spider. Horror explodes in my chest as I retch again, this time bringing up bile. The yellowish liquid hits the floor and mixes with the blood, creating a murky color that makes me heave again.

"You're crazy." I can't help but say it.

The person rises from their place on the floor by the door and hovers over me. Their long hair threatens to brush the top of my head as I cower away. I don't want to see what that mouth looks like after eating the bloody spider—I can't take it. I drag my body along the floor, whimpering and shaking with fear and pain. Every inch I move back, my attacker matches with a small footstep. Their foot thumps on the floor, echoing through my mind like a death knell.

"Please! I don't want this!" I shout, voice growing louder with desperation.

A booming knock sounds at the door, breaking the silence in the bathroom. We both freeze.

"Babe? You okay in there?" calls a voice from outside.

Matthew. My partner. I didn't know he was home.

I try to scream that I'm not okay, that I need help and I need it now, but my vocal cords fail and nothing but air escapes my lungs. I just spoke—my voice can't be gone. The hand on my good arm flies to my throat. Matthew knocks again, but I am powerless to whatever is happening to me. The only silver lining is that Matthew will not leave. If I don't respond, his worries will prevail and he will break down the door if he has to. I just need to buy myself a few more moments of continued silence. I kick a leg forward, trying to knock something from the sink counter, but the force holding me to the floor wins out and I cannot move. My body shakes with effort and the person in the bathroom with me can tell what my goal is.

They reach a quick hand out and snatch up my hairbrush, making sure there is nothing on the edge of the counter to clatter to the floor. They look at the brush, cocking that curious head once more, and start brushing their hair. Normal people brush along the sides or the back, but this person brushes from the center of their head straight down the middle of their face. I've never seen someone brush their hair like this and it feels creepy. They brush and brush in complete silence, and I can't do anything but watch.

"Babe? Do you have headphones in or something? I'm getting worried..."

My gaze snaps back to the door, and I am desperate for Matthew to quit wasting time. I need him to barge in and save me from this demonic attacker. The person stops brushing their hair and sets the brush down at the back of the sink, far from my reach. They turn around so I can only see their back. They sweep their hair back and away from their face, and I need to see what they look like. I can't move past the need to know. My legs remain glued to the floor as I lean far to my right, trying to catch a glimpse. If I could see their face, maybe

I could make sense of this nightmare. The person clears their throat, and I realize with shock they are about to speak. They haven't spoken before.

"I'm fine, honey, sorry!" the person calls out and my blood freezes in my veins.

Their voice is my voice. Exactly my voice. How is that possible?

"Alright, I'll get started on dinner," Matthew calls, and I hear his footsteps recede from the door. My salvation is leaving—all hope dashed to the floor like my blood.

My attacker turns back to me with calculated slowness, like something not of this world. I try to shriek, but nothing comes out. My voice is as gone as my legs are stuck. They take a small step toward me. This time, I am ready for them. I am not going down without a fight. I can see the knife on the floor out of the corner of my eye, but don't dare look at it. I don't remember them putting it down, but it doesn't matter. I want to have the upper hand. As the person crouches down, I can tell they are staring at me from behind that thick hair.

While they are in mid-crouch, I reach out my good arm and shove them to the ground. They land with a thud on the floor, and I hope Matthew heard it, and I hope he comes running back up the stairs. I can't rely on him though—I only have myself. Desperation floods my system as I reach out for the knife, but my attacker moves with preternatural speed. They grab the knife and snatch it from me, holding it to their chest like a precious artifact. This is it. This is the end. I can feel it in my bones, in my cells.

As if my body knows the truth, I collapse to the floor, shoulder hitting the tile with a sharp bang. The person stands above me and that chuckle resumes, low in their belly. They grab my unmarred arm by the hand and I am powerless against their grasp. All I can do is watch as the blade of the knife lowers toward my skin. I can't look away as it slices me, creating a twin of the wound on the other arm. My blood pours down this arm in a rapid flood before slowing down. I look at the other arm and see the blood is slowing down there as well.

I'm dying.

My attacker sets down the knife on the floor with a gentle but firm hand, signifying a job well done. I don't think about grabbing the knife—I don't think about fighting my way through this. A quiet resignation has taken over my mind. I like how it feels. I don't need to live—I need to know who is doing this before I die. I will never know anything again, but I need to know this. The person sits on the floor beside me and puts a gentle hand on my hip. My arms somehow find the strength to reach up and finally part that curtain of hair. I look with a devouring eagerness at their face and see that it's me. It's my face staring back. I experience the most intense emotions of my entire life—confusion, sadness, devastation, and then understanding. As the world around me grows dark and my breath becomes shallow, I look into my own eyes and realize what I have done. I am my own attacker. I have taken my own life.

Ravens' Retribution

by K.L. Allister

My legs were criss-crossed in my chair as a trickle of water ran down the back of my neck. My black and gray robe bunched up and cradled my naked skin like a warm hug. The magenta tinge of my Pinot noir bounced off the reflection of my wine glass; the sound of it filling, an orchestral ovation for my ears' pleasure. With a light sigh, I readjusted the towel holding up the sodden tangle that was my hair. *At least it was clean.* The glow of the computer screen mirrored in my hazel eyes, the loud *ping* of a conversation bubble grabbing my attention.

Nine o'clock. Right on time, as usual. His large head—the focal point of his profile picture—took center stage at the top of the conversation box. The matted scruff of his beard—more like a chinstrap—compounded my disgust for him, if possible. The glasses he wore, big rimmed and bulbous, contributed to his 'studious and learned demeanor', as he so *frequently* reminded me. *Fucking gag me.*

I rolled my eyes, sipped my wine and read his message: "Hey baby girl."

The grimace that usurped my facial features could not be understated. I abhorred this man. I loathed his very existence. So why were my fingers flying across the keyboard, egging him on, pandering to his feeble attempts at courting? I'm a woman with unbridled rage in my heart and a plan to match, that's why.

One year ago, my sister Diedra was followed to her car after work. The restaurant was always open late, and she had the misfortune of closing up shop that night. This man, this *monster,* decided to act on his baser instincts and assault her. He took advantage of her in her own backseat under the dim light of shoddy headlamps. Diedra was deeply traumatized and wouldn't even talk about the incident until two months later.

She described him vividly—the same man whose picture I'm staring at right now. And although the police had incredibly accurate descriptions, nothing came of it and we hadn't heard of any developments in a while. *Typical.* That's when I made this online profile: Jaela Howell. Insert random bimbo headshot here, cheesy inspirational quote there; a couple pictures of my *actual* cat, Zephyr, and I started hunting.

He wasn't hard to find. Dead, stale eyes and a slight twinge of a smile—devious and predatory—in damn near every picture. The thought of his hot breath on Diedra's nape made my skin crawl. 'Jaela' has been his focus for the past six months, slowly wrapping him around her finger, biding her time and planning. Always planning.

"Got sumthin for u," his bubble read. "Check ur phone."

Another loud *ping* caught my attention—a multimedia file pulled up on my phone. Another unsolicited picture flaunting his pygmy-sized, pinprick of a dick—that makes about ten now—with the caption 'been thinkin' about u'. Truth be told, I've been thinking of him, too. But not in the way he was thinking of Jaela, that's for sure. As appalled as I was, the next phrase he typed out set my blood ablaze.

"When u gonna give it up to big Chet?"

The same fucking thing he said to my sister the night he violated her. My fist clenched and my knuckles whitened, nails burrowing into my palm. The eloquently—and strategically slutty—response I typed out suggested a meet, disguised under the term 'date', and lined the fabric of my words with subliminal promises of pleasure. Being the brutish, troglodytic, deplorable man he was, he fell for it. Hook, line and fucking sinker.

Another gulp of wine, another guised message sent to my sister's rapist. It made me sick, all of it. Why her? Why did he feel the need to exercise his ill-perceived dominion over women *that* night with *my* sister? I found myself often wishing it had been someone else. As morose and morbid as it was, me and Diedra are blood, as are all the girls. This insufferable bastard made his choice a year ago, and I will do everything I can to ensure he fucking meets his end.

Nearly twenty minutes after the conversation began, I messaged Chet and feigned exhaustion. A few kissy face emojis and a wink sealed the deal. I knew I had him right where we wanted him. Before signing off, we established the venue for Friday's 'date', a dive bar fifteen minutes from my house.

"You pick, baby," he'd said to me.

Aww, what a fucking gentleman.

I glowered at the screen, wanting to drive my hand through the monitor. Some semblance of my brain's dissonance willed the theoretical strike to land on his jawline or collapse his piss poor excuse for a dick. Call it wishful thinking. The only thing keeping my balled fist from kissing circuitry was the fact that I would need to replace it myself.

I felt my breath stagnate in my lungs as I arose from my chair. The stem of my wine glass greeted the ceiling, the last bit of the ruby red gliding down my throat. I freed my reddish brown hair from its towel, meandering to my closet, letting the wine warm my belly. The robe's fabric brushed against my nude skin as I pulled it off. With a light mewl, I ran my hands down my milky curvature and giggled to myself.

As I donned my silky pink pajamas, my phone—the real one—rang loudly from my desk. A contact photo filled the screen: a pitch-black raven with its wings sprawled, an embossed 'K' underneath.

I pressed the green button and walked back to my closet, a large cardboard box on the ground before me.

"Karma," I answered, fiddling with the box. "He took the bait. We're on for Friday. Get the girls ready."

An alleviated sigh. "Oh, good. Madam Corvus and the Krowned Lich were asking about you."

"Did they say anything about Chet?"

"We...brought it up," Karma replied hesitantly. "Let's just get him here, then *they* will be the judges."

Understandable. "And what about Diedra? Are they cool with me bringing her along?"

"Is *she* okay with coming?"

I pursed my lips as I curled my fingers around cold American-made steel. The .38 Colt Python's leather grip invited my touch like a long-lost love. Its trigger, a wicked mouth yearning for fleshy contact, longing for release.

"She will be," I responded. "She needs this."

"Okay," Karma breathed, unsure. "Send the deets to the group chat and we'll be ready."

I hung up the phone and put my revolver back in its box. Anger pulsed through me as my sister's recollection of that night played over in my head, on repeat. My lip twitched in abject frustration—furious at the police for not taking her seriously; at society for empowering men and pushing the narrative that women are mere objects to be played with at their beck and call; and furious at the thick cloud of nonchalant ignorance subservient women exacerbate with their self-deprecating decisions.

I pulled myself from my thoughts when I realized I was crumpling the box's sides.

What I planned wouldn't change the world, and it certainly wouldn't re-stitch the fabrics of society. But it would bring one cretinous motherfucker down. The ladies from the *Femella Corax* are in my corner—the Krowned Lich, Madam Corvus and the ever-hungry Black Mother incoming. Although Diedra is only a hatchling in their eyes, this closure is something she needs, and something I will provide as her older sister.

My name is Jade Slater. And I will see burning feminine rage consume the life of my sister's rapist.

The car's brakes squealed as it rolled to a stop. My eyes shifted side to side, from car to car throughout the busy parking lot. The throng of patrons migrated toward the neon sign in the bar's window. Faint memories flooded back, reminding me that Chet drives a navy-blue Nissan Altima. The high lamps flickered, providing minimal reprieve from the waxing twilight.

I craned my neck downward to my lap to read a text from Karma:

"We're here. We got your back. *Corvi in aeternum.*"

The cult's creed revitalized my slowly-sapping confidence. I joined the *Femella Corax* four months prior and never committed a sacrifice to the Black Mother. Chet would serve as both retribution and dedication; his life, the penance.

My phone pinged again. A message from Chet.

It read, "Hey bb, I'll be there in five."

Now was the time to steel myself. He defiled my little sister. Every time I looked at his profile picture, a dormant rage became unmarred again like a freshly-sliced wound, seeping deep into my pores, threatening to ravage my very constitution. He is not a man. He's weak. A demented animal in need of euthanasia, nothing more.

Who knows how many other women he's victimized? Two...ten...*twenty*?! Men like this don't rape just once. They don't just get their rocks off and call it good. My heart bled for those he's hurt; all the betrayal, rage, hatred and disgust boiled at the surface—a neglected dinner pot billowing clouds of steam. My lips curled in revulsion at the thought of him traipsing around the internet with impunity, as if he got away with it. Boys will be boys, they'll say.

"Boys will be fucking dead," I mumbled to myself, vigilantly scanning the parking lot.

Bright headlights beamed through the windshield into my eyes. As it passed, I let out a low snarl: Nissan Altima, navy blue. A part of me wanted to ram the side of his car at full speed, my own injuries be damned. No, that left too much of it up to chance; maybe he gets a couple scratches, minor concussion. No—patience and methodical action, that's how I get this done.

"Just pulled up, baby. Where r u?" the text message read.

Congealed bile crept up my throat. *Composure, Jade.* My thumbs tapped my keyboard with a loud clacking.

"Be there soon. Ten minutes," I responded.

My eyes swiveled to my right, where the ladies were lying in wait, ready to play their part. Chet exited his car and ambled into the bar, his gait filled with moxie and self-confidence. So sure of himself—no doubt lubing up his inhibitions with a stiff drink while he waited for Jaela. Might as well let him enjoy his last drink, right?

I drew my breath in, filling my lungs to capacity before steadily pushing it back out. *Do or die, Jade.*

The clacking of my keyboard bounced off the cab walls. I hit send as I slammed the car door behind me, walking over to the poorly-lit area of the parking lot. My message read:

"Fuck! I just pulled up, but I locked my keys inside my car. Come out and help me?"

Playing to his ego and a certain, unspoken hope in the back of his—and every man's—mind that he would be 'rewarded' for his chivalrous behavior, I knew he couldn't pass up my damsel-in-distress routine. Men are so malleable. Give them a flicker of hope that they'll get laid, and they're putty in your hands.

I examined the syringe of diazepam in my hand, the faint yellowish hue reflecting off the plastic tube. The slate gray van was right next to the Subaru I camped out at; silhouettes shifted inside the metal chassis, waiting for my knock.

My back turned to the random car; I feigned fiddling with the handle. The crunch of gravel sounded behind me, growing louder with each footfall. I ignored it—I needed him closer.

"Jaela," he probed. "Jaela, is that you baby? Here, let me help you."

I felt the light grip of his hand on my shoulder. The syringe sunk into his neck as I turned around to face him. Teeth ground, I bore holes through him with a wrathful stare. He raised his hand up to his neck, bewildered and disoriented.

"You're...not Jaela," he whimpered before darkness encased his consciousness.

"Pretty fucking perceptive of you," I muttered. I reared back and spat at him, thick spittle hitting him in the face.

I knocked twice on the side of the van. Instantly, Karma's beaming face greeted me; three other ladies of the Order clung to seats behind her—Jenna, Moira and Kiera. All their eyes settled on the worthless pile of human shit at my feet, then quickly clambered out to collect our prey. Once inside, they threw him down onto the leathery backseat.

Karma cupped my cheek, her eyes soft and filled with concern. "Are you okay?"

"I will be," I replied, my heart still racing. "Let's just get this motherfucker to the Sanctum."

My fingers gripped metal. Knuckles cracked as I clenched tightly. I nodded to Karma.

She doused Chet in ice cold water, his awareness returning immediately. His body thrashed and he yelled at the top of his lungs.

My features twitched. "Wakey wakey, you piece of shit."

Muscles were ordered into motion as my fist crashed against the bridge of his nose. Cartilage bent and cracked; the brass knuckles I wielded instantly carved a tight gash between his eyes. The red grew more intense; ruby-colored globs slowly trickled down his face.

"What the fuck?!" he screamed. "What is all this? Where the fuck am I?"

We remained silent, waiting. The confines of the vast, ornate atrium shot up toward a vaulted ceiling, six pillars splayed out from the center. There, Chet was rendered immobile, bound to chains feeding four thick metal rings ensconced in the two closest columns. In the center of the floor, a large elaborate carving of a raven graced the stone. The ceiling boasted the embossed visage of our Black Mother. His blood traveled down his hung head and dripped down onto the raven's sculpted eyeball.

His cries for help continued. So did our silence. Two wooden doors at one side of the sanctum creaked on its hinges, opening slowly. Three figures emerged, one dressed in white robes and the others clad in black. The ceremonial hood worn by the figure in white obfuscated her true features, except for the radiant green eyes behind a bird-like cutout. Those in black wore white plague masks, their long noses protruding outward. The expressions on our faces brightened, as we have become all too familiar with the three luminaries that stood before us. We all bowed in reverence.

"What the actual fuck is all this?" Chet bellowed. "Halloween was last month, you stupid—"

His words were cut short as one of the figures in black hurriedly clasped his large hand around his throat. The chains that held him rattled against the liminal space between flesh and stone. His robe's fabric receded as he pulled in a large breath, taking in Chet's scent. A disgusted groan escaped his mouth.

"It smells of deceit and treachery," he said, his words a blanket of safety, a searing hot knife weaving through room-temperature butter. A hidden blade pressed against Chet's neck. "If you speak out of turn in the presence of my Lady again, your tongue will be wrested from your mouth...to start. Nod if you understand, vermin."

Chet struggled to draw air into his lungs, but managed a strained nod. The figure released Chet and we couldn't help but smirk as he sucked in heaping gulps of oxygen.

The woman's gaze regarded Chet, her gnarled fingers lifting to the black-robed man. "I am Madam Corvus, prophet of The Black Mother, Matriarch of the *Femella Corax. Corvi in aeternum.*" We repeated the words. "You have upset my Krowned Lich, as well as six of my followers. They seek retribution against you."

Chet was petrified to speak. His chilled silence tasted sweet on my tongue.

The Krowned Lich dropped to his knees and rubbed the side of his face against Madam Corvus' abdomen. He whispered indistinct prayers in the direction of her pelvis. Our Lady continued.

"These brave women have brought their grievance to these great halls, for the Black Mother to preside over." The Krowned Lich stood, taking his place at her right. "They seek penance, sacrifice. What say you?"

Chet did not respond.

"Speak!" the other figure—The Dark Inquisitor—blurted. "My Lady asked you a question!"

Chet gulped. "I--I don't even know these women. Wh—what could I possibly have done to them?"

The Krowned Lich scoffed, pinching his knife's edge between his fingers. "Insolent cretin."

"Karma, bring in our hatchling," Madam Corvus commanded.

Karma bowed her head in affirmation, then pushed the wooden doors open. Moments later, she reappeared with Diedra in tow. Chet's eyes grew vast at the sight of my nineteen-year-old sister.

That's right, motherfucker.

Madam Corvus turned her head toward my sister and outstretched her hand. "Come, child."

Diedra approached, hesitant and scared at the glimpse of her abuser.

"Your sister and the members of her dark flock seek justice on your behalf," her eyes scanned our faces. "Present your case before our Mistress. She alone will decide if vindication is yours to claim."

I listened as my sister recounted her story. Each detail burrowed into my psyche as if my ears heard it for the first time. My body mimicked the retelling of how she felt. The shiver of my spine, my forehead sequined with droplets of sweat. The knotted tangle of my insides threatened to eat me alive. It felt like I was there beside her as he violated her.

Tears slowly drained from Diedra's eyes, then she embraced Madam Corvus, only to join us in front of Chet. Her head cocked to the right and shot him a malicious glance.

"Your crime has been professed to the Black Mother," Madam Corvus proclaimed. "Now we await her decision."

The two dropped their heads to their chests, hands clasped and fingers interlaced; Madam Corvus raised her hands to the ceiling, invoking our Mistress. Seconds felt stretched throughout the expanse of time. Chet coughed behind us, still reeling from the Krowned Lich's impromptu brachial treatment. We interlocked our own fingers—Diedra's in mine and mine in Karma's—as we whispered the Prayer of Retribution:

Oh, our Dear Black Mother
Hear the words we've come to know
Ardent Mother, protector of the flock
Our hearts are brimming with woe
Before us stands our aggressor
Deserving of his dues
Allow us to bestow our wrath
Wholly cleansed of Evil's ruse
Our wings are spread and ready
Justice and retribution come
Your flock begs you this sacrifice
Corvi in Aeternum

Silence filled the sanctum. Diedra glanced at me, worried. Here we were, wanting to put an end to the hurt, and if not accepted, Chet would escape justice again. I squeezed my sister's hand in solidarity.

A low hiss came from the sculpted face above. An opaque mist—black in color—exuded from the stone visage. Relieved smirks played at the corners of our mouths. Karma shot me a mischievous and knowing grin.

"Our Mistress has spoken," Madam Corvus' voice boomed. "Retribution is granted. How it is exacted is of no importance. We will give you your peace to dole out penance."

Chet flailed about in his chains again, knowing his time was short.

Madam Corvus, the Krowned Lich and Dark Inquisitor turned toward the wooden doors. Just as she was at the threshold, Madam Corvus cocked her head over her shoulder.

"Oh, and girls?" We all perked up, providing our full attention. "Do clean up. You know how I hate messes."

We all chuckled softly. Karma ambled after them, broke off to the right and dug into a big steel chest. She collected *something* from it, something I couldn't see, then the others followed. They egged me on, urging me to 'pick something from the chest'. I walked over and peered into the ancient container.

From what was left, I could gather it was full of weapons. My gaze shifted back to the girls, and sure enough, I was right. Karma stood by, twirling throwing knives between her fingers. Moira whipped around a chained cat-o'-nine-tails in an arching flourish. Kiera donned coiled chains around her forearms, pulling and testing their durability. Jenna and Dakota both brandished a paring knife and cleaver, ready to cleave and bleed Chet where he hung, suspended.

My eyes fell upon a ball peen hammer. That paired with my 'knucks', and this motherfucker didn't stand a chance. I gripped the hammer and returned to the group. We turned to face Chet, terror enveloping his facial features and his limbs shaking like errant tree branches. Pungent urine soaked his slacks, an acrid puddle forming below him.

"So, how we doing this?" Karma asked me. The knife's ring twirled around her finger in rapid rotations. "One at a time, or we could bum rush him all at once."

I want his pain drawn the fuck out. He doesn't get the privilege of this ending quickly. For my sister, for me, and for all the women he's hurt. We will be his reckoning. We will be searing hot, unadulterated feminine fucking rage.

"One at a time," I replied monotonously, devoid of emotion. "Nice and slow."

Karma simply smiled and said, "You got it." She paused and looked at my sister. "Diedra, you wanna kick us off?"

My sister was quiet. Nerves wracked her body, not sure of what was going to happen next. I know because I felt the same. It was as if a tough question was asked and no one knew the answer. Nobody wanted to be the first to raise their hand. Nobody except Karma.

"No? Okay, I'll do the honors then."

She tossed one of her knives in the air, flipping end over end, and caught it by the handle upon its descent. Before I could blink, she flicked her wrist rapidly, sending the blade careening toward Chet. His screams echoed through the chamber as it found its new home in his left shoulder. The next knife sliced through the air with a loud *thwip* and embedded itself in his right leg. *She's purposefully avoiding vital areas.* Two more sunk into his other shoulder and leg, a dark crimson pooling underneath his beige pants.

"Chet, Chet, Chet," Karma began, "You thought you got away with it, didn't you?"

His breathing grew ragged, panicked as he beheld his rather skewered state of affairs. "I told you. I—I don't know any of you bitches! I don't know what the fuck you're talking about!"

Karma slapped him across the face *hard*. The chains that bound him took a second to cease their movement.

"Oh no, we're not playing *that* bullshit. I saw your fucking eyes when Diedra walked in." A tested hatred tugged at the marionette strings holding her voice. "Everything she told us was true, wasn't it Chet?"

"No! I don't know what the *fuck* she's talking about!"

Karma grabbed the handle of the knife in his shoulder and twisted. Tissue and ligament tore, the blood's flow increased and his mouth let out an otherworldly screech. I scrunched my nose at the sounds.

"Tell. The fucking. Truth," Karma seethed.

Chet sighed, panting to try and regulate his breathing. "Okay, okay. Yeah, I recognized the girl."

Karma twisted again. "Not fucking good enough."

"AHH! Alright, alright...Yes, everything she said was true." He heaved a guilty breath. "I raped her."

Another strike—this one close fisted—landed against the top of his cheekbone., blackening his eye in mere moments.

"That's all we needed to know," Karma said, emotionless. "Moira, you're up."

Moira dragged her weapon of choice along the stone; the clattering of sharpened blades reverberated against the masonry. She stood about ten feet behind Chet and arched it above her head. As it came down, the cracking of the whip resounded, followed by agonized shrieks as the blades tore into his back. Deep lacerations formed, smaller bones crunched under the weapon's pressure, and scarlet drained in sheets down his spine.

Moira brought the cat-o'-nine-tails down again and *again* and **again**, ignoring his futile cries for help. After five or six repetitions, the flesh on his back was reduced to shredded chicken, mushy and bloody. The gashes overlapped, more skin coming away in long, thick strips. Moira giggled to herself, proud of the work she'd put in.

"Well, that was fun," Moira said. "Who's next?"

Kiera stepped forward with her chains, facing him head-on. The grimace on her face was a perfect example of 'if looks could kill'.

"So, you like preying on women, huh?" she inquired with a snarl.

Red foam trickled out of Chet's mouth, accompanied by low groans and pained breaths.

"Please," he wheezed. "I didn't..."

"Didn't what?!" Kiera yelled. "Didn't mean to stick your piss poor excuse for a pecker where it didn't belong? Better yet, where it wasn't *wanted*!"

Her last word was accentuated by the thick metal slamming against Chet's midsection. Another blow fractured his humerus, eliciting more well-deserved pain. She crept behind him and wrapped the chain around his neck, pulling and yanking, edging him closer to Death's door but stopping *just* shy of the threshold.

Kiera improvised, grabbing one of Karma's knives.

She looked over her shoulder and winked. "I'll get this back to you, babe. Promise."

Karma just shrugged, unbothered.

Kiera coiled the chain around Chet's right ankle, then jammed the knife between the links. Her forearms bulged as she rotated the blade over and over again, like a tourniquet turned torture device. She kept going until she heard an audible *snap*, breaking all the bones within. Chet threw his head back in agony as Kiera repeated the process on his left side. His feet dangled lifelessly, barely contained by the shackles.

"There," Kiera said, admiring her handiwork. "Now, even if you *do* leave here with your life, you'll be a crippled mess." She grabbed his shirt and pulled him in close. "Then you'll *really* know what it's like to be less-than."

Jenna and Dakota were next, flashing their cleaver and paring knives, respectively. They boasted them in front of Chet, the glint of silver reflecting in his corneas. A thin line of bloody drool dangled from his shock-laden lips.

"Jenna?" Dakota asked, her chin propped up with her fingers. "What is that phrase circulating around the social webs?"

Jenna smiled a toothy grin. "Ohhh, I think you're referring to 'dead men don't rape'!"

Dakota nodded. "Thaaat's it...but we can't kill him yet. No, no, no. But we *can* take away his favorite plaything."

The two women chuckled to each other. Then Dakota's demeanor flipped on a dime.

"You think your dick is God's gift to women, don't you?" She slapped him twice, as he was fading out of consciousness. "Hey asshole, I'm talking to you. How many women trusted you, just to have you besmirch their friendship with your actions? How many brave women have had their confidence shattered by you 'taking what you want'? One, two, twelve?!"

Chet murmured something under his breath, too low for any of us to hear.

"Speak up, bitch, I can't hear you!" Jenna snapped.

"I—just a few, I guess," he confessed. "I—"

I looked over at Diedra, stoic and unnerved. My rage boiled over and I screamed at him. "One of them was my little sister, you sick fuck!"

I made a beeline for him, my fist curled around the metal of my brass knuckles. Karma grabbed me by the shoulders and held me back.

"You'll get your chance," she told me. "I promise."

Her eyes were warm, inviting. The same they'd been when I first sought out the coven. I trusted her, and she trusted us. My breathing slowed and I crossed my arms.

Dakota whispered in his ear, "You can't rape if you have nothing to rape with." She pulled away from the side of Chet's head with a lascivious smile on her face.

"Please, don't," he cried, tears meshing with sweat and snot. "I—I'll do anything. I'll give you money, just let me go! What do you bitches want?!"

Dakota held her knife by the blade and offered it to him. "You could always cut it off for us. Saves me the trouble."

His mouth agape, Chet only stuttered. His words fumbled in his throat.

"Fuck no!" he finally managed to utter.

"Suit yourself," Dakota shrugged. "But I will warn you, I *am* legally blind in one eye, so my cuts might not be exact." She paused, then laughed. "I'm just fucking with you. But seriously, I *am* going to cut your fucking dick off."

Chet writhed desperately, trying to wear out his restraints. All to no avail. His pleading grew in volume—a cacophonous petition for mercy. I smirked as Dakota unfastened his belt, dropping his pants to his ruined ankles.

A humiliating, raucous orchestra of laughter escaped our lips. I've seen the pictures, but it truly was more pitiful in person. Diedra turned away, more than likely reminded of that fateful night. Dakota wielded her paring knife and grabbed the base of his dick. She dug into the soft flesh and dragged her knife down the length of his stretchy shaft, revealing muscly tissue, thin tubing and glassy cartilage. The steel flicked outward from his slit; a spray of ruby dashed against the gray of the stone floor. Blood poured steadily from the wound, quickly sopping his pants below.

His yells reached higher decibels, sending twitches of pain through my eardrums.

"Precision is key, you see," Dakota mused. "Enough to maim, but not enough to kill. And *that*," she pointed at his groin, "you sure as shit won't be using that ever again."

"And this should distract you from what's going on down there," Jenna chimed in, holding out one of Chet's bisected ears. She cackled as she spoke into his disembodied ear canal. "Can you hear me now? I'm going through a tunnel!"

Her cleaver came down and chopped the other ear from his head and met the floor with a wet *slap*. Gore and plasma drained from the concave hole. Diedra was behind me, puking. I couldn't really blame her. This was some intense shit...but we signed up for this. We intended to sacrifice to the Black Mother and we were exacting our vengeance, one piece at a time.

"Jade," I heard Karma say. "Why don't you and Diedra bring us home."

I looked deep into her eyes, then shifted my gaze to Chet behind her. His mangled form became more of a testament to maternal fury than of a human. My face twitched with a small sense of joy. I nodded, then took Diedra by the hand as we faced her rapist.

"You violated my little sister," I declared to a barely-conscious Chet. "I posed as Jaela to hunt you down. You are here because of me. Your body is in its current state because of me. Women put you here, and I want you to remember that." I sucked in a deep breath and took in the sanctum's beauty. "I kept telling myself this is all for Diedra, and that I wouldn't enjoy it. But I gotta say, I have a feeling I'm gonna like this next part a whole lot."

I brandished my 'knucks' and blasted him in the jaw. A few teeth clattered loudly on the floor, spittle and blood following closely behind. Another blow opened up a gash on his forehead, then another broke his collarbone. Three more successive hits to his torso evoked a crescendo of cracked ribs. *Music to my fucking ears.*

I gripped the hammer's wooden handle and drove its head right into his decimated pelvis, adding insult to injury as his body absorbed the blow like some morbid punching bag. Crunches and cracks provided me with the audible feedback I needed to ensure maximum damage. Chet released a myriad of anguished moans and unintelligible noises while I ravaged his body.

Out of breath, I took hold of his bloodied face, his tattered lips pursed together. "I...am Jade Slater...a Tier Three Raven of the *Femella Corax*," I stopped to recoup my breath. "And you are *done* fucking with women. We are *not* your property, we are *not* inferior, and we sure as hell shouldn't be fucked with."

I turned on my heel to see my sister staring at me. A tiny hint of a smile teased at her mouth. As depraved as it was, she knew we were doing this for her, to bring her abuser to justice where our system failed us. The Black Mother knows justice and will grant retribution to those who deserve it. I saw that in her eyes—the cleansing flood of absolution.

I reached behind me, into my waistband. I curled my fingers around cold American-made steel. The leather grip invited my touch; its trigger longed for release. I handed the gun to Diedra.

"Put an end to all the trauma," I told her. "Complete the sacrifice and send his foul soul onward, wherever it may land. Find the strength to end it, Dee-Dee."

She took the revolver from me and looked it over, appraising its weight in her palm. Aloft and shaky, Diedra pointed it at Chet's head. The bullet chambered as his chest rose weakly.

"Puh—plea—"Chet wheezed, more blood gushing from his lips. "Ple—please. I—"

His begging was abruptly silenced and replaced by the gunshot that followed. The song of my .38 Colt Python bounced loudly off the walls of the atrium. Chet's head exploded with hot, red gore and grayish brain matter. His neck snapped back due to the sheer force, then lolled to meet his sternum. My gun fell from my sister's hand and rattled on the floor. She cried as I pulled her into my arms, the ladies of the *Femella Corax* enveloping us.

Two days passed since we killed Chet. Diedra and I visited Madam Corvus' home to see his body propped up against a thick willow tree in the garden. A lone raven sat atop his head and plunged its beak into his left eye. Vitreous fluid spurted as the eyeball slid down the bird's gullet.

I surveyed all the carnage we inflicted on this man: his mutilated back and pelvis, his earless head, his broken ankles and the hole in his head. The aperture in his head was black and discolored, serving as a stark reminder to anyone who dares cross me and mine—the lengths we will go to set things right are immeasurable. The women of the *Femella Corax* are strong, I am strong, and I am honored to be counted among them.

The afternoon wind scooped Diedra's dark brown locks up and off her forehead, highlighting her strikingly beautiful features. I smiled at her, and her at me as we took one last look at what remained of Chet. The raven squawked, seemingly in approval as we embraced.

"I'll always be here for you," I whispered in her ear.

We walked out of the garden rejuvenated, unburdened of a great trauma. Chet may have skirted the law, but the Black Mother and her followers had other plans. I can finally have peace knowing he's gone, and I know my sister can too, eventually. Healing begins where the hurt stops, and our hurt ended with him.

Acknowledgements

First, a huge thank you to my Chaos Scribes for your endless love, encouragement, and belief in me and my slightly unhinged idea for this project. Through the ups and downs of writing—and life—with or without this book, we've built something really special together. I am so proud and incredibly grateful for you all. Thank you for trusting me with your work; your trust and friendship truly mean the world to me. I am humbled to be the one to publish all of us together—many of you for the first time.

To Gage Greenwood—thank you for bringing us all together, shoving us into a room, and throwing away the key. You believe in us and that is irreplacable. You are the World's Best Soduku Grandma/Applesauce/Douche Faucet ever.

To Sally Feliz, thank you for your sharp eyes and thoughtful feedback. You helped make this something we can all be proud of, and I can't tell you how much I adore and appreciate you.

To the Witches Three—may our late night margarita and meme sessions last forever.

And last, but not least, to you, the reader—thank you for picking up this book. I hope it speaks to you in some way. I hope you discover a favorite new author. Your support means the world.

About the Authors

SAVANNAH R. FISCHER

Savannah R. Fischer is the permanently exhausted pigeon in charge of two well-loved chaos gremlins. When not with her family, she can usually be found in her cave, wrapped in an oversized blanket and dreaming of spinach puffs. She wants to show her gremlins that they can do hard things, even when it's scary, like pulling the wrong lever and ending up in a pit of alligators. No llamas were harmed in the making of her works of horror.

Derek Thomas

After 55 years of living in the urban jungles of Dallas/Ft. Worth and Houston, Derek now dwells in a small central Texas town with his wife of 18 years and two precocious French Bulldogs; where he survives on tacos, whisky and Coke Zero. When not writing, he loves to cook, garden and, of course, read and watch horror. He is particularly fond of Asian horror and Scanda Noir films and shows. His first novella, Blood Brawl, was released in July of '24 by No Pants Publishing to excellent reviews, with a sequel planned along with two more releases in 2025. As well as a story in another anthology soon. Derek is a proud liberal and continues to fight the good fight for any and all marginalized citizens, with a focus on supporting the LGBTQ+ community.

Kate Reedwood

Kate Reedwood was born a blue-eyed, blonde-haired cherub with the heart of a goth. It beats beneath the floorboards of the box she lives in in Canada. She rarely goes outside, preferring the company of words to that of the sunlight. Sometimes you can hear her cackling at night while she conjures imaginary friends. If you do… run.

ANDY EDGE

Andy Edge lives in the desert with his dogs and a few tiny frogs. A horror enthusiast to his core, he devours everything from slashers to supernatural thrillers, though his writing delves deepest into psychological terror. When he's not crafting stories to unsettle readers' minds, he's probably watching horror films, reading horror novels, or planning his next haunting tale.

Kristal Shanahan

Based in Kansas, Kristal teaches high school literature and writes spooky stories late at night. If she isn't encouraging her dogs and cat to play nice, she's spending time with her family. Kristal enjoys reading and writing in several horror tropes, mostly everything is palatable. Her credits include a story in *Book Nerds' Book Review 1 (Community Anthology)*, a story in *Scorned Anthology,* and self published stories; *Fiery Mable, Clara Knows Possession,* and *A Twisted Malevolent Christmas.* In spring 2025, she will release her first collection and her debut novella in summer 2025, Waves of Evil Descent, an urban legend story. Kristal plans to keep writing for the unforeseeable future, producing many more works after her upcoming retirement in education in 2026.

Kimberly Nicole

Kimberly Nicole lives in the USA, deep in the south. She grew up in the 90's as an Army brat and had the privilege of traveling to many different states and countries. She loves all animals, the color red, and all things horror. She uses fear as a form of pain relief to combat CRPS, fibromyalgia, and other personal demons. It has been a lifelong dream of hers to write and publish a book one day and she finally decided to reach for that dream at the crisp age of 34. She hopes you enjoy spending time with her words.

AJ Humphreys

AJ Humphreys is an emerging author of thrillers, horrors, and mysteries. The four-part Season of The Monster saga has served as his debut within the publishing world. Not one to fear going against the grain, Humphreys ditched the corporate world in 2021 for the food service industry, permitting him more time to focus on the haunting tales his mind conjures. When AJ isn't writing, it's a safe bet he's outdoors and his best pal, Kobe The Husky, is somewhere nearby.

Joseph Murnane

Joseph Murnane lurks at the mouth of a cave off the banks of the Eno River in Durham, North Carolina, with four hellish animal companions and an eldritch queen of terrifying beauty. They say you can see him there just before dawn, but only out of the corner of your eye, and only if he wants to be seen. He can be reached via blood dance, or if the trials prove to o difficult, email works too. Jmurnanehorror@gmail.com

SVEA NIETZKE

Svea Neitzke is a newbie writer who loves horror. She lives in Milwaukee, Wisconsin with her daughter, husband, ancient black cat, and dorky Doberman. She graduated from Alverno College in 2011 with her B.A. in English. This is her first full year back in her old state after living for 2.5 years in Rio Rancho, New Mexico. Even though she loves city life, nature will always have a special place in her heart.

David K. Slater

David K. Slater goes by many names, he likes it when you call him Slater The Writer or Mr Night-Terrors. He writes, wait, why am I talking in third person? I'm not The Rock. I write what I like, I write what scares me, what makes me laugh, and what makes me cry. I've been told that if I write for myself I'll find my audience. So what about you? Are you my audience? My debut novel Air Conditioned Nightmare, is coming in 2025. Gage Greenwood said "It does for customer service calls what The Shining did for Hotels". Get ready. You are not re ady.

Jacinta Rae

Jacinta Rae lives in the New England area with her husband, cats, dogs, and chickens. She has a passion for all animals and would never pass up an opportunity to help one in need. She loves to be surrounded by nature and still gets spooked easily in the dark. Her hobbies vary with her interest and most nights are spent snuggled up with a good book.

Dylan Wells is a full, 100% human being (promise!) who spends her days witnessing the real-life horrors of late-stage capitalism and nights dallying in fictional worlds. She now lives in Wisconsin with her cat and a constant sense of dread. You can read more from her in From the Ashes' anthology, *Hootenanny Horrorshow*, Crystal Lake's *Hotel Macabre, Vol.1*. You can follow her on Instagram @DylanDisappeared and friend her on Facebook at facebook.com/DylanDisappeared.

Mel Kitching

Mel Kitching (she/her) is a new indie horror author residing on the border of NY and PA. Mel has been a lover of all things spooky and macabre since she was a child. When she isn't writing, you can find her behind the chair at the hair salon.

Ali Toothman is a horror reader and writer from Southern Illinois. She is a mom to two and a coal miner's wife. You can usually find her with her nose in a book or writing on her laptop, surrounded by her 3 giant dogs. She is an active horror community member and loves supporting indie authors. Her love for writing and telling stories runs as far back as she can remember. She has done various types of writing throughout her adult years and has made up many stories for her younger siblings. Ali fell in love with horror when she was 8. The feeling of being scared drove her to want more of it in her life, whether from movies or books. She began writing her first collection at 30 and can't wait to bring those nightmares to readers.

JULES TERRY

Jules Terry is an Arizona cryptid and crazy cat lady. She spends as much of her free time with her nose in a book, writing, or making art. She is the mother of four lovely, little gremlins, and keeps a menagerie of pets ranging from cats, dogs, to chickens with her husband. Her love of horror started young and kept her parents thoroughly concerned. She enjoyed renting creature horrors from Blockbuster, in addition to the bloodiest anime she could find. When she was not living out her bog witch dreams, she would curl up with books by Stephen King, Dean Koontz, or Dostoyevsky or play video games, mostly Diablo or World of Warcraft. Not much has changed, except her TBR has grown significantly.

Chris Heinicke

Writing has always been in Chris' blood, but it wasn't until 2007 when he decided to put his fingers to his keyboard and only take 8 years to write his first book. After releasing his third book, he met his co-writer, Kate Reedwood, by chance, which set off a series of science fiction books, then a change of genre to horror. Living in the large coastal town of Coffs Harbour, he lives with his wife and three kids, but is always ready to take on the next writing challenge.

DENVER WHEELER

Denver Wheeler (they/them) is a non-binary author from Williamsburg, Virginia. They studied psychology in college and graduate school, and run a small mental health counseling practice as well as actively practicing as a therapist. Denver's literary work deals with different aspects of mental health and how trauma can affect us all. In their spare time, Denver enjoys reading, spending time with horses, and being with their husband and child. Denver is a proud member of the LGBTQIA+ community and incorporates this pride into their writing. Denver's work can be seen as a contest winner on Crystal Lake and their debut novel DEAREST DAUGHTER published by Blue Fortune Enterprises.

K.L. Allister

I'm K.L. Allister, extreme horror and splatterpunk author. I probe my sick and twisted brain in order to bring abject depravity to lovers of the macabre and deranged. Tell your therapist I sent you.

Jyl Glenn

Jyl Glenn is a writer, editor, formatter, anthologist, and medical writing coach. She works as a legal nurse consultant to support these habits. Her lifelong love affair with horror began at a very early age when she was left unattended in front of the TV the weekend Poltergeist debuted on HBO. She soon figured out she could read any book she liked as long as she hid out at the public library—even if the librarian deemed it not to be age-appropriate for check out. Jyl's mission is to help get new writers published and curate as much chaos as possible. She was born and raised in New York and now lives in Tulsa. When she isn't dabbling in the macabre, she's probably...ummm. Nope, that's it. Follow her on IG @_delightfully_unhinged_ or on Facebook at Jyl Glenn Writes.

9 798991 990806